ONE TEQUILA

An Althea Rose Novel

_____

TRICIA O'MALLEY

Lovewrite Publishing

"In Florida we salt margaritas – not sidewalks."

Chapter One

"BUT I'M QUITE certain Bitsy would wish to speak with me," the woman across from me sniffed and clutched a folded silk handkerchief with a perfectly monogrammed E on the corner. The point of her chin rose as she looked down her nose at me.

"Mrs. Evanston, I've already explained this – I'm a psychic – not a medium," I sighed as Mrs. Evanston's eyes steeled up and her shoulders braced.

"Well, I'd say that you're certainly misleading people with your little psychic shop if you can't even talk to Bitsy for me." Mrs. Evanston narrowed her eyes at me. I could already read the threat in her mind: she would be contacting the Better Business Bureau and by lunch, she'd be tearing my reputation to threads with her Ladies Who Lunch club. Mentally rolling my eyes, I plastered a smile across my face.

"The reason that I don't advertise being a medium is because it's so incredibly draining for me," I began, lying through my teeth. "However, for you, I'll make an exception."

A muffled snort from a screen to my left almost had me cracking a smile but instead, I stayed focused on my client. Hope had dawned in Mrs. Evanston's eyes as she leaned forward, hands pressed into the purple velvet of my table.

"You can? Oh, oh, just...can you tell me if she is safe?" Mrs. Evanston breathed, staring into my glass scrying ball on the table.

I closed my eyes and counted to ten, doing my best to get an image of Bitsy from Mrs. Evanston's thoughts. A puffball of a white cat popped into my head, so I went with it.

"Her coat is just as stunning as it was in life – I see her walking proudly," I said, keeping my eyes closed and praying that I had hit the mark.

"Ohhhh," Mrs. Evanston breathed and I snuck a look to see her with a hand over her mouth, a sheen of tears making her eyes glint behind her glasses. Her hair, the perfectly blue-gray rinse favored by the elderly set on Tequila Key, bobbed as she nodded.

"She was really proud of her coat. Bitsy was a show cat, you know," Mrs. Evanston said.

"I can see she carries herself as such. She is wonderfully happy and has told me that her only concern is for you to find peace with her passing," I said gently, using my *de rigueur* explanation when clients insisted that I contact a loved one.

No matter what, it seemed that when people heard psychic, they thought I could do anything.

Magic even.

I'd leave that to my best friend and business partner, Luna Lavelle, the one who had so gracefully snorted from the other room of our Luna Rose Potions & Tarot Shop tucked on a sleepy street in Tequila Key, Florida.

"You know, Althea Rose, your mother may be the famous one, but I think you've inherited her gift," Mrs. Evanston said, rising to shake my hand with a smile. I scanned her thoughts and all I got was pleasure, so as far as I was concerned, the reading had been a successful one.

I checked my moral compass and decided as white lies go, it was a minor one. People only come to psychics for two reasons – to find out if they will be okay and to find out if someone they love will be okay. I turned my palm over to look at the $1 tip she had pressed into my hands. I had to laugh. Though the rich in this town liked to flaunt it with country club passes and fancy houses, in all reality they were stingy to the core.

Pressing my hands to my eyes, I willed back a headache that threatened to dull my thoughts.

"Drink this," Luna said, interrupting my brief debate over closing shop for the day or not.

I smiled at her as I took whatever potion she had mixed up for me and held it to my nose. Luna slipped into the chair across from me and waved an impatient hand at the drink.

"Althea, I know your tastes by now, you'll like it."

Vanilla mint soothed my throat as I sipped the cool liquid and my head cleared instantaneously. I tilted the now empty glass at her in a salute.

"You should sell this."

Luna sighed and tucked her stick-straight blonde hair

behind her ear. My best friend and business partner was my antithesis in every way. Airy, elegant, with a sharp business mind and mile-long legs, Luna made her living breaking men's hearts and helping the down and out of Tequila Key.

That whole white witch thing didn't give her much room on the "bound to help" area of her life, I thought. Much like the Hippocratic Oath – when Luna saw suffering, she sought to fix it.

And didn't that just make her a better person than I?

Annoyed with where my thoughts were going, I refocused on Luna.

"Bad day?" she asked.

"Could be better. Drinks on me tonight!" I sang, holding up the dollar bill that Mrs. Evanston had left me with. Luna's warm chuckle flowed across the table – a light and lilting sound. I'd seen men turn at thirty paces and backtrack just to meet her after hearing Luna's laugh.

"Oh, like Beau ever makes us pay," Luna said with a smile, speaking of Beau Redford, our mutual best friend and owner of Lucky's Tiki Bar.

"It scares me to think what our tab could be." I pushed away from the table, unaccountably antsy, and paced my side of the store.

The Luna Rose Potions & Tarot Shop was a combination of our names and a clash of our personalities. From the outside, a whimsical coastal cottage with two front doors welcomed our clientele. The weathered white siding with stars and moons painted across the wood just added to the charm that was peculiar to this section of Tequila Key.

But – depending on which door a client chose to walk through – two different worlds awaited.

My side, the Tarot & Psychic shop, was set up precisely as one would expect a tarot shop to be. A few years ago, I'd gotten a bee in my bonnet about dispelling the myth of un-professionalism in the tarot world and had transformed my shop into a waiting room similar to a lawyer's office. Soothing gray tones with light pink accents, a potted plant in the corner. Luna had scoffed at it and to my surprise, my business had all but dried up.

I've since learned not to mess with people's expectations.

Now, my side screamed "PSYCHIC! LIVE READING!" louder than a flashing neon sign on the window. Miles of red and purple crushed velvet was draped across the tables and chairs, while crystals, statues, and incense cluttered the shelves that lined the room. A privacy screen blocked my clients from the other side of the shop and a combination of Luna's new age music and her magic kept clients in the potion shop from hearing the dark secrets shared in mine.

I loved my little shop, I thought with a smile. A skeleton in the corner sported a Ramone's t-shirt and Day of the Dead candles lined my altar. It fit me to a T.

I flipped my hand over to check the time on my watch, the face turned inside my wrist so as to allow me to discreetly check the time during my readings. Below the watch, an intricate tattoo wound its way up my inner arm, holding both an evil eye design and Celtic warrior protection symbols.

One could never be too safe.

"I like your color this week," Luna said, gesturing to my hair. I stopped my pacing and turned to stand in front of a small ornate mirror to study my reflection. Curls in every shade from deep brown to neon pink rioted around my face, subdued only by a jeweled headband with a skull that I'd tucked in there earlier in the day. Reaching up to fluff my curls, I tilted my head.

"The pink does pop my eyes a bit," I said.

"Those cat eyes of yours pop no matter what," Luna said dryly.

I suppose they do, I thought as I widened my green eyes that naturally slanted at the corners. A flowing silk maxi dress, the color of the sea at dawn, covered my body and made me look like one tall cool cylinder of water. Well, water with a few ripples, I thought, eyeing a generous butt that the flowing dress didn't fully conceal.

"I love this dress," I decided and turned back to smile at Luna.

"You say that every time you wear it," Luna said with a smile, standing and stretching. A dainty white camisole and white linen slacks covered her thin frame. White linen slacks that didn't dare wrinkle, I might add.

"I have my ways," Luna said, reading my thoughts.

"I can't do white. I never understand how you can wear white every day and not get stains on it," I grumbled.

"Maybe you should try paying attention to where you are going and you won't end up with stains so much," Luna said gently and motioned for me to follow her to her side of the shop.

"We closing out for the day?" I asked, and turned to switch a small beaded lamp off behind my table.

"Unless you have any more appointments?" Luna's voice floated back to me.

"Nah, and I doubt we'll get a walk-in today. Tuesdays are typically pretty slow," I murmured as I went around the room clicking off lamps and throwing the bolt in the front door on my side. I stood at the window for a moment, peering out into our sleepy street, my anxiety still high.

"It's nothing," I reprimanded myself and slid the blinds closed, grabbing my beaded, fringed, slouchy boho bag.

Stepping from my shop to Luna's was like going from Walmart to Neiman Marcus. Elegance oozed from every whitewashed corner. Luna had gone with upscale beachy, with a predominant theme of white, gray, and gold show-cased throughout the room. Large reclaimed wood tables and shelves held hundreds of bottles, each with a gold top and a fancy white-and-gold label. Luna believed that presentation was everything and I couldn't argue with her, as her potions and elixirs were in demand around the world. At times I wondered if she thought my side of the shop was dragging hers down.

"Why do you have that look on your face?" Luna asked, squinting her blue eyes at me, one small line marring her perfect forehead.

"I just am always amazed that you're willing to slum it with the likes of me," I said, gesturing to the beautiful display of crystals on a table in front of me.

"Knock it off, you bitch," Luna swore, knowing that curses coming from her delicate mouth would get me chuckling.

"You're the bitch," I said, cracking a smile at her.

"See? This is why we are best friends and perfectly

suited to do business together," Luna said, pointing a finger at me as she moved behind her counter and began to total her receipts.

I traced my hand over a chunk of amethyst on the table.

"Our shops are just so different," I said, unable to drop it for some reason.

"Which is why they work. They are complementary to each other," Luna began, sighing as she put the receipts down and waited for me to finish, knowing that I would keep interrupting her math until I got it out.

I shrugged, and picked up a small citrine crystal and held it to the light.

"I know. I guess sometimes I just feel like I'm dragging you down. You've got all this beauty and light over here," I said, gesturing with the citrine, "and I'm all dark and crushed velvet over there."

Luna crossed her arms and studied me more carefully.

"What's really bothering you? This has never been an issue before."

"Nothing, I don't know, I…" I shrugged and put the citrine down, unsure why I was feeling insecure, unsure of where these emotions were bubbling up from.

"Althea. We can't be the same. We should never be the same. It isn't light and dark. It's just that our powers and our very essences are so different. This…" Luna swept her arm out to the shop, "would be nothing without you. You are one of the top psychics in the country. You bring in as much business as my light working and potions do. And don't even get me started on your beautiful art," Luna said, gesturing to where my underwater photographs lined her walls. "We're a team. And in more than just business. This isn't like you at all to question that," Luna said, her head tilted, receipts forgotten as she studied me. I could feel her mental probe as she tried to get a reading on my feelings.

"I'm worried," I blurted out and then stopped, wracking my brain for why.

"Why?" Luna crossed her arms and watched me, taking my concerns seriously.

"I don't know. I've been anxious all day. But when I try to get a grasp on what or why…" I spread my hands in front of me and raised my shoulders, "nothing. I see a gray mist of nothing. I don't know what that means."

Luna came around the counter and began to pace her shop, mimicking my moves from a few moments before.

"That's highly unusual. Now I'm worried. Can we call Abigail?"

Abigail Rose is my mother, one of the most sought after psychics in the world, and currently tucked away in Greece doing a reading for a dignitary. Or was it a movie star? I could never remember.

"You know how they are when they travel," I said, thinking with love of my parents.

"Yes, completely off the radar," Luna murmured, wrapping a strand of her hair around her finger and tugging it.

"I'm sure it's nothing. Maybe just that time of the month." I shrugged, wanting the conversation to be over.

"Nice try, Althea, but I know you," Luna said, picking up the receipts again. "Let's meet at Lucky's in an hour. It'll give you time to feed Hank."

Hank, my parents' Boston terrier, had become a fixture in my home as they traveled the world.

"Yeah, he's probably getting antsy by now. I'll give him a quick run and then meet you over there. Um…just call me when you leave here, okay?"

Luna paused.

"Now you really have me worried."

"It's fine. I swear it's fine. But until I know why I'm feeling this way…just…put your protection spells up. And carry your knife," I said, reluctant to leave.

"Great, Althea. Now I'll never finish these receipts. You know what? I'll count them tomorrow. You can bike me past my place. Okay with you?"

I blew out a breath and nodded, feeling the tension in my shoulders relax.

I held up the citrine again before slipping it into my purse.

"Add this to my tab."

Chapter Two

"SEE YOU IN AN HOUR," I called, ringing the bell on my beach cruiser bike as I pedaled away from Luna's swanky condo that always made me a little on edge to hang out in. Her design style was echoed there, with a lot of white on white and long windows that let in the light.

I'd have stained the couch with red wine by now if I lived there, I thought as I circled my bike and waved to Mr. Roberts sitting in his rocker on the front porch of Fins, the local everything store.

Tequila Key is a small town with big city aspirations. Often skipped over by the tourists on their way from Key Largo to Key West, Tequila Key had gone through a small re-birth in the 70s. In a bid to attract more tourists, the mayor at the time had thought it would be fun to rename the town from Whittier Key to Tequila Key, thus enraging the Whittiers, whose family had been some of the first to live here, and ensuring that we would never be taken seriously by anyone, ever.

At the entrance to town, just a marker off the highway, a huge sign proclaimed, "Tequila Makes it Better." Whoever's genius idea it had been to erect that had driven the final nail into the coffin on getting any actual tourists to come further into the city. Instead, cars full of people would pull off the highway, take their picture by the sign, and continue on to the party town of Key West, leaving Tequila Key an all but forgotten stop on their journey.

This relative obscurity worked just fine for me, as well as for a slew of creative types who had wandered their way here over the years, pushed out of the other Keys by rising land prices and expensive tourist restaurants. The rich had found their way here as well, for those craving a sleepier waterfront lifestyle while still getting the most bang for their buck. An invisible line seemed to form through the town, with old Tequila Key being a colorful assortment of houses clambering over each other for space and New Tequila – that is, the newly renamed Port Atticus – housing the Ladies Who Lunch with manicured lawns and gated subdivisions.

And, somehow, it all worked out just fine, I thought as I rode my bike past a series of shotgun-style houses, boasting porches painted in a myriad of colors, with large plantation shutters ranging along tall front windows. My house was the last in the row, giving me an unobstructed view of the water from the side that wasn't connected to the rest of the row.

I smiled as I heard barking from my house. I had worried that I was the annoying lady on the block whose dog barked all day while she was gone, but my neighbor swore that Hank only barked when I was coming home.

Some days I took Hank with me to work, but he was a little high-energy for some of my clients.

I got off the bike and wheeled it towards my faded blue house, the porch painted bright lavender with white trim work. An Althea Rose bush climbed a trellis on the side, its blooms offering a cheerful welcome. It was still undecided whether my parents had named me for the rose bush or the Grateful Dead song. Knowing them, it was probably a combination of both.

I loved where I lived, the color and cacophony of the houses on the street reminding everyone that even though we were still connected to the mainland, we were islanders at heart.

Two ears poking up from beneath the windowsill were all I could see of Hank before I slid the key in the door and pushed it open, immediately crouching to stop him from racing past me.

"Hank! You miss me, buddy?" I said, laughing as Hank ran in circles around me, jumping up to lick my face, before tearing around the house.

"Got the crazies?" I called as I heard him snorting and skidding over the wood floors as he ran, tearing through the large open layout of the first floor. Hank was a traditional black-and-white Boston and twenty pounds of pure love and sass. Part of me suspected that my parents had never adopted him for themselves, but instead to keep me company while they traveled.

A beep from my purse alerted me and I dug into it, pulling my phone out and swiping the screen to see an email from my mother.

"Speak of the devil," I said, and perched on a paisley-print chair in screaming pink and aqua tones. It didn't match anything in the house and I loved it.

Having a blast in Greece, my love. Your father loves the Ouzo. Did a marvelous reading for Eminem. I see him doing big things this year. I'm worried about you. Do me a favor please and be careful? Kisses to Hank!

A picture accompanied the email, bringing a smile to my lips. My parents beamed happily at me, my dad in rumpled khakis with spectacles slipping off his nose, his face red from the sun. He had his arm around my mother, a statuesque redhead in a flowing pink caftan. The blue of the Mediterranean stretched behind them and my heart tugged a bit, missing their nearness.

My parents had done their best to steer me away from a traditional upbringing. In doing so, they'd become more than my parents to me; they were also my best friends. Mitchell Rose, my father, had been a professor of music at Boston College when Abigail Henry had walked into his class and taken a seat in the front row. She hadn't been enrolled in the college, but had gone there to meet him based upon a psychic vision in a dream.

The rest, as they say, is history. In a matter of years they had moved to Tequila Key, where my dad published professional papers on music history while teaching classes on the side at the local community college. Because of the accuracy of my mother's predictions, her reputation had grown so quickly that money wasn't an issue and they lived life as they pleased. Bringing me into the world had been a natural extension of their love and I'd been a cheerful and exuberant child – one who danced in the yard to the music my father played while learning tarot cards at my mother's knee.

My teen years had been saved from the awkwardness of trying to figure out if a boy liked me by the undeniable fact that I had inherited more than my mother's curves and sharp mind. Being a psychic at sixteen certainly came with its own advantages, and the residents of Tequila Key hadn't blinked twice when I'd followed in my mother's footsteps.

Hank whined at the back door and I glanced across the room. Most shotgun-style houses were called that because each room butted up against the next, separated only by a wall. When I'd bought this house, I'd gutted the lower level and added the top floor, using a small inheritance from my grandmother to do so. The result had left my first floor as one big open floor plan and had allowed for three bedrooms and two bathrooms on the second floor.

I loved my space even though I knew the chaos of it made Luna itch when she came over for Wednesday wine nights. Because I had one open room, including the kitchen, I'd shoved all sorts of furniture, lamps, and knick-knacks into the space, creating conversation corners and nooks. It was crowded, colorful, and there was always a place for someone to sit – from the 18th century imperial bench to the bright red metal ottoman. I'd painted my walls a pale gray and then promptly covered them with my other secret passion, underwater photography.

"Okay, I'm coming," I called to Hank, the lingering warning in my mother's email making me nervous as I walked to the back door and let Hank out into the back-yard. A long cedar fence I'd painted a deep maroon lined one side of the yard and separated my yard from the rest of the houses. Instead of closing in the yard though, I'd left it open to one side.

To my secret piece of heaven, I thought with a smile and laughed as Hank immediately raced down to the small stretch of beach that had come with this house. Sure, I paid extra for the ocean frontage, but it had been worth every cent. I had to have a piece of the water for myself. Water, unlike anything else in this world, called to me, soothed me, was my solace and my joy. I needed to be near water as much as I needed my next breath. From the front of the house, it looked like the yard ended at a rocky outcrop-ping. It was my private slice of paradise that very few knew about, and I liked to keep it that way.

Hank did his business and bounded back to me, a stick in his mouth. Checking my watch, I reached down to tug the stick, knowing that I'd need a good twenty minutes of playtime to satiate my active dog.

"Let me grab a glass of wine, Hank, and I'm all yours," I called, popping back into the kitchen to grab a glass. I could walk to Lucky's from my house so I'd have enough time to play with Hank. Looking down at my dress, I considered changing but then shook my head.

"You love this dress," I reminded myself and stepped back outside, moving to sit on a low couch that I had placed under the large bamboo fans that hung from my patio ceiling. Hank ran up again and I tugged the stick from his mouth, knowing we would repeat this sequence another seventy times or so.

My life was practically perfect and just the way I wanted it I thought as I sipped my Chianti. My mother would point out the glaring absence of a man, but I liked to think of this time as my independent period. I sniffed and shot my nose in the air before taking another sip of wine.

Hank barked and ran in circles while the waves lapped at the shoreline, the sun beginning its slow descent into the water.

It just doesn't get any better than this, I decided.

Chapter Three

I TOOK MY time wandering the quarter mile to Lucky's. Not only was the humidity almost oppressive, but I knew that Luna had a tendency to always arrive ten minutes late. I'd long ago stopped meeting her on time, knowing that I would just sit there fuming. A warm glow from the setting sun caressed the houses, making everything look old-timey and quaint. I waved to the locals who sat on their porches, observing their children playing in the front while exchanging gossip over spiked sweet teas. I loved this time of night in Tequila Key. Music – and there was always music – bumped from an old boom box on someone's front porch and the smell of Cajun food filled the air.

"Althea!"

"Miss Elva," I called, veering from the street to stand at the bottom of a weathered porch. A large woman wearing a flowing multi-colored robe, with skin the color of honey mixed with cocoa, laughed down at me.

"You set some people on the right path today, Althea?"

Miss Elva said to me, cocking her arms on her generous hips.

"Always," I said cheekily, laughing up at her.

"I've got something for you," Miss Elva said, the smile slipping from her face and her eyes going serious. I immediately stiffened.

Miss Elva was legendary around all of the Keys for being a high-ranking voodoo priestess. She was often called to remove curses and to perform blessings. When Miss Elva got her serious face on, I listened.

Miss Elva reached in her pocket and pulled a small cloth pouch out, holding it out to me. I paused, pulling my hands behind my back, and shook my head at her.

"Uh uh, gris-gris? You'd better tell me why you think that I need it," I said, dropping my shields and trying to read her mind. She batted her hand at the air, effectively brushing off my attempts to scan her brain.

Like I said, Miss Elva was nobody to mess with.

"I cracked an egg today. Blood in the pan. Take it. Please," Miss Elva said, brandishing the pouch at me again. Tentatively, I reached out and took the bag from her, looking down at the faint etchings of words that ran across the soft cloth. The punch of power was unmistakable and I shivered to think about what was in the bag.

"Is it bad?" I whispered, wishing for the first time in my life that my sight would be clear for my own sake.

Miss Elva shook her head yes. Then shook her head no.

"I can't say. Just keep this with you. You're one of the good ones," Miss Elva said before retreating back onto her porch, the dark corner seeming to envelop her.

Great, I thought, shoving the gris-gris into my purse, now the voodoo priestess is warning me too. Luna and I needed to have a serious chat tonight if we were going to get to the bottom of this. Worry clung to me as I turned the corner to the main drag of Tequila Key.

The street was as busy as it could be for a Tuesday night in what passed for downtown Tequila. Bars and restaurants clung to the beach, fighting for every precious inch of space, while the opposite side of the road housed a few gift shops, a bookstore, and an ice cream parlor. Lucky's commanded the best spot on the beach, at the end near where I walked, jutting out just a bit on a cliff. It allowed the bar to have almost unadulterated views of the water and of the town. Large wooden tiki gods lined the path up to the thatched roof building, and tiki torches blazed every few feet, their purpose twofold – ambience and to keep the bugs away.

Beau had bought Lucky's sixteen years ago when we had just graduated high school. His father had died suddenly, leaving him money, and freeing Beau from any expectations his family had for him to follow the good ol' boys' path. Beau had come out to me when we were twelve while reading gossip magazines at lunch. In turn, I'd told him about my psychic ability. Neither of us had batted an eye and we'd been best friends ever since. Lucky's, formerly a snack shack, had transformed under Beau's careful guidance into the most popular bar and restaurant in town, with a not-so-secret after-hours gay club in the basement. The police looked the other way on the after-hours party because Lucky's drew the most tourist activity in town. It was a win-win for everyone.

"Thea!" Beau called from where he was blending a drink. A group of women sitting at the bar turned and scanned me, envy etched across their faces.

Oh, you poor things, I thought as I smiled at Beau. He was handsome in a way that made everyone fall in love with him, never venturing too far into metrosexual dress as did the men that he typically favored. Instead, he affected a perfect blend of Miami Beach club and surfer casual cool. With a killer body, and closely cropped blond hair, I'd seen more than one woman get tripped up over him. It always flustered Beau when a woman came on to him, but his kindness in letting them down almost always turned them into life-long customers.

Again, another friend who was better than me, I thought with a snort. My mouth was known to get me in trouble on occasion.

"Hey, beautiful, love the pink," Beau said, gesturing to my hair as he leaned over to kiss both of my cheeks.

"Thanks, I was in a mood," I said, and slid onto a stool, relaxing into the ambience of the bar. Teak wood booths clustered the walls, while smaller bamboo tables held court in the middle of the room. Lamps made out of spiky puffer fish ranged across the ceiling and fish netting was hung artfully across the walls. The bar was open in an almost 360-degree circle, but thin mosquito netting kept the bugs from bothering the clientele. It was the perfect blend of campy and welcoming, and the service was excellent.

Beau slid a mojito in front of me, knowing my preference.

"How was your day?"

"You know, channeling dead cats, the usual," I said with a wave of my hand.

"Ah, changing lives I see," Beau said with a smile, holding a finger up to me as he turned to help another customer.

Alone for a moment, I decided to drop my shields and see if I could get a sense on whether any of the foreboding that was hanging over me could be emanating from someone here. Batting away the lusty thoughts of the girls at the bar, I allowed my mental eye to scan the room. A red swath of anger washed over me and I tensed, trying to find its owner. My eyes settled on a round man holding court at a long table, his cheeks pink with laughter, his stomach popping past his suspenders like a biscuit can that had exploded.

Theodore Whittier.

Rolling my eyes, I snapped my shields back into place and focused back on my drink. Theodore Whittier – of the Tequila Key Whittiers thankyouverymuch – was a man with his hand in everything. He was on the board of just about every committee, owned several different busi-nesses, and had never met an opinion that he didn't like – so long as it was his own. My skin crawled as his laugh, designed to draw attention to him, boomed across the room and made me want to throw my soggy napkin at his face. Everything about Theodore was ooze-worthy. It wasn't entirely out of the norm for him to have an undercurrent of rage either, as he was typically up in arms about some-thing. It wasn't an uncommon sight to see Theodore blus-tering to the local sheriff about one thing or another. The epitaph on his tombstone would probably read "Get off my lawn."

"What's up with Theodore?" I asked Beau when he came back to me. Beau raised an eyebrow in question.

"He's pissed about something but not showing it," I clarified.

"Ah. It's either that I won't comp him his bill or that I didn't pick his site for my new restaurant."

I all but dropped my drink.

"Your new restaurant?" My voice went up about five octaves. It wasn't easy to keep something from a psychic, let alone your psychic best friend.

"What new restaurant?" Luna asked as she took the stool next to me. I glanced over to see her slim body perfectly ensconced in an impeccable mint green sheath, coolly lovely as usual.

"Great dress," I said before turning back to Beau. I jabbed my finger in the air.

"Talk," I demanded.

"Well, it's just been an idea swirling around in my big ol' brain," Beau said, leaning over the bar, exaggerating his drawl. I reached over and smacked him in the arm, bouncing lightly in my seat in excitement.

"You're killing me – don't make me read your mind," I threatened, swirling my striped straw around in my drink. I raised my eyebrow in warning, causing Beau to laugh.

"It hasn't gotten that far or I swear I would've told you more. I've just been toying with bringing an upscale seafood restaurant to Tequila Key. We've a lot of middle-of-the-road type restaurants, but aside from the Shore

Club, there's nowhere to take a date for a nice dinner." Beau shrugged.

"That's an excellent idea. I do get sick of driving up to Key Largo for fancy dinners," Luna said.

"I don't. Oh wait, that's probably because millionaires don't come through and woo me like they do you," I said, smiling at Luna to soften the snark in my voice.

"Speaking of, I've got a man for you," Beau said casually and I straightened, bringing my finger up to point at my chest.

"For me? Not her?" I asked incredulously.

"Yes. You. Now, check out tall, dark, and oh-my-god-do-I-wish-he-was-gay sitting next to Mr. Blowhard," Beau said, nodding slightly towards where Theodore slapped his palm on the table and harassed his waitress for more drinks. Sitting next to him was a man I had missed in my earlier perusal, and I shit you not, he took my breath away for just a moment.

"Whoooo, boy," I whispered.

"Mmhmm," Luna said, her face by mine as we gazed at the handsome hunk that God had bestowed upon us this fine evening.

At least six feet of well-muscled man leaned casually back in his seat, his thick dark hair complementing his tanned skin, light eyes tracking the room. He reminded me of Channing Tatum and I gulped as those light eyes landed on me.

Luna and I turned so fast I almost knocked my drink over.

"Don't make me hose you two down," Beau chuckled, flicking an ice cube my way.

"Who is that?" I breathed, my face burning from being caught staring. I was dying to look at him again, but I couldn't bring myself to. I was afraid that I would melt right on the spot, slipping from my stool to the floor in a puddle of lust and embarrassment.

"That, my beautiful friends, is the newest investor in my restaurant. If good looks aren't enough, he's rich enough to buy Tequila Key should he be so inclined. His name is Cash Williams, no pun intended, and he's a sight for sore eyes in this small town," Beau said, reaching for my glass that I had slurped dry after getting an eyeful of Cash.

Of course the hot rich guy's name was Cash, I grumbled to myself.

Beau held up my glass in question.

"No, I'm diving in the morning," I said, cutting myself off from any more alcohol. I planned to squeeze two dives in tomorrow before my first client at eleven. It was time for me to update my online store and blog with more underwater photos.

"Where's Cash from?" Luna asked, interest lacing her voice.

"Wait — more importantly, why are you saying he's for me when he could have her?" I asked, honestly confused. Luna and Cash would make an astounding couple, all purebreds, sleek and shiny. I was more of a mutt that would be up for a good cuddle on the couch.

"Stop it, Althea. You're stunning," Luna said immediately and I reached out to squeeze her arm. My best friend, always championing for me.

"Right, I get it. Statuesque goddess and all that, but

seriously, why for me?" I asked Beau, pinning him with my stare.

Beau shrugged. "I don't know. Instinct? Bartender intuition? I'll introduce you guys when they get up from dinner. You'll like him. On top of being drop dead yum, he's actually an interesting guy and so far doesn't seem to be full of himself."

"Who's the guy next to him?" Luna asked and I turned again, pretending to casually glance through the restaurant. I'd missed the handsome guy sitting next to Cash as I'd been momentarily blinded by Cash's raw punch of hotness. The man to his right looked to be Cuban or Puerto Rican, with warm brown skin and brown hair slicked back from his face. A gold chain glinted from the deep V of his silk dress shirt.

"He looks like a Miami club guy," I said, turning back to Luna.

"He might be; I think he works with Theodore," Beau said.

"He's cute," Luna offered.

"You think? He's a little too sleek for me," I murmured, refusing to look back at the table – then immediately looking back at the table. This time, Cash met my eyes and I felt my cheeks flush. Feeling bold, I nodded at him and a smile split his handsome face.

"Oh lord," I breathed, turning back to bury my face in the seltzer water that Beau had pushed across the table.

"Maybe take him in small doses," Luna said, running a soothing hand down my arm.

"I'd take him in any dose," Beau observed and I snorted.

"Okay, enough with all this, tell me where you are thinking of setting up this restaurant," I pleaded, desperately wanting to change the subject.

"Well, you didn't hear it from me, but Luca is closing his deli," Beau said, leaning over and keeping his voice low.

"No!" Luna and I both said simultaneously. Luca's Deli had been serving up sandwiches and the best pickles in town since I was a kid. I couldn't imagine Tequila Key without him.

"There are other investors who are looking at the space, though, because it has a prime beach spot. I'm not sure if we'll get it. That being said, I have two other options for spaces, so I'll be okay either way."

"Wait, but, why?" I asked, still focused on Luca making the decision to leave. He was as much a staple of this town as the faded Tequila sign out by the highway.

"Supposedly, Luca met a special lady friend. Special lady friend wants to travel Europe. Luca didn't think twice about it." Beau shrugged again, and then moved to fill a drink order.

"Luca's leaving, wow," I said, turning to Luna. Sadness crossed her beautiful features before she snickered.

"Luca wants to get lucky," she said.

"Shhh," I said, shushing her. "That's like talking about our grandfather!"

Her shoulders shook with laughter and I couldn't help but join her.

"Good for him," I said, lifting my seltzer in salute, before clinking the glass against Luna's. She sipped her

Moscow Mule, served in a copper mug, and then straightened and turned to me.

"Okay, let's get back to why we came here. Tell me what you think is going on," Luna said, her eyes tracking my face.

"I don't know. I really don't. But, get this – my mother emailed me a warning. And…" I reached in my purse and pulled out the cloth bag that Miss Elva had given me. Luna drew in a sharp breath. You didn't have to tell a witch what a gris-gris bag was for.

"Two warnings," Luna breathed.

"I know. I just wish I could see why. I just have this super heavy sense of something…I don't know. It makes me antsy. But I'm getting no visuals," I said, pointing at my head for emphasis.

"Let's do a seeing spell at the shop tomorrow when you get in. We'll see if we can clear the fog out," Luna decided.

"Yeah, I could use the help," I said, ashamed to admit that my typically formidable gift had failed me.

"It's okay, hon, you can't always see everything. Even your mom misses things once in a while. If she had seen something important, she would've given you details," Luna said.

"You're right, Abigail rarely holds back," I said, feeling somewhat comforted. No way would my mom have seen something that was going to harm me and not give me a heads up. Unless…

"But it goes against her rules to interfere with a vision," I said, reminding Luna of one of the rules that most psychics, including myself, practiced. No matter the vision, one shouldn't interfere with Fate.

Because Fate always finds a way.

"I suspect she'd break that rule in your case," Luna said dryly, taking another sip from her mug. I watched a bead of water drip down the side, missing her dress.

Naturally.

"So we wait," I said.

"We wait."

Chapter Four

"HELLO," A VOICE – like whiskey-laced sin – said at my side and I felt a small ripple of lust in my gut.

I turned to see Channing, I mean Cash, leaning casually on the bar, his demeanor open and friendly, his eyes assessing us.

"Hi," I squeaked.

"Hi, I'm Luna and this is my friend Althea," Luna said, jumping in to cover my awkwardness.

It was hard for me to look at him. My heartbeat had picked up and I was certain that my pulse did a *rat-a-tat-tat* tempo in my wrist.

"Nice to meet you both," Cash said. "I'm Cash Williams and I've just moved to Tequila Key."

"Moved?" I said, finding my voice, turning to look at him for real this time.

"Yes, moved. Is that okay?" Cash said lightly, crinkling what I could now see were gray eyes at me. Of course they were gray. My favorite. I sighed.

"Why the sigh?" Cash said, calling me out.

"You're too good-looking for your own good," I blurted out and then slapped a hand over my mouth.

"Thea!" Beau chided from across the bar, but Cash chuckled. I'm quite certain that every woman in the bar went a little lightheaded at the sound.

"I could say the same of you," Cash said, fixing his eyes on me.

"Me?" I said, whipping my head around to look at Luna. "Her, you mean."

Beau shook his head at me in disgust from across the bar.

"Well, both of you are lovely, of course," Cash said gallantly.

"Ignore her," Luna said, "you'll get used to her mouth."

I blushed even more furiously, thinking about Cash getting used to my mouth.

Beau choked and turned away, but I could see his shoulders shaking at Luna's choice of words.

"I find her to be charming," Cash said smoothly, covering the double entendre of Luna's words easily.

"So, Cash, you're an investor?" I asked brightly, trying to push thoughts of my mouth on Cash's from my brain.

"Among other things," Cash said with a smile.

"What other things?" I immediately demanded. I needed to get a read on this guy if he was going to be working with Beau. My protective instincts kicked in and I narrowed my eyes at Cash, all business now.

"I own a few restaurants straight out. I've invested in others. I've worked in private security as well, which pairs nicely with protecting investment properties and such,"

Cash said, a dimple winking from his cheek. I studied him and dropped my shields.

And immediately blushed.

The man wasn't lying.

About his business or the fact that he found me charming. I was surprised to find a healthy lust directed my way. Snapping my shields back up, I trained my eyes back on Beau where he was serving a customer.   .

"Good to hear. Beau is the best in this business. And his heart is pure gold. Remember that," I warned.

Cash held his hands up.

"Hey, I know that. Why do you think I want to invest in him? He's great."

"You know he's gay, right?" I said, wanting to see how much that would matter to Cash. Not everyone always picked that up right away about Beau.

"I'm aware," Cash said, raising an eyebrow in confusion.

"Just checking. Some people have issues with that," I said simply.

"My brother's gay. And he's my best friend. No issues," Cash said, raising his hands in the air.

"Did I hear you say you have a gay brother?" Beau piped up from across the room, proving that he did, indeed, hear everything in his bar.

Cash laughed and turned his head over his shoulder.

"Yes, and he's single. I'll bring him down next month," Cash called and Beau fanned his face, causing Cash to chuckle again.

Was there anything wrong with this man?

Remembering who his dining companions were, I looked at Cash again.

"Why were you eating dinner with Theodore?"

"He's on the board of, like, everything in this town. We'll need permits and such. It's a good idea to make nice," Cash said, reading me perfectly.

"Sounds like you are a very smart businessman," Luna said, and reached for her purse. "I'll just be on my way."

I turned and grabbed her arm.

"No, don't go. You've only had a drink."

"I want to prepare stuff for our thing in the morning," Luna said quietly and shot a quick smile at Cash. "Nice to meet you." She waved to Beau on her way out and was gone faster than I could say don't leave me with this hot man who I have no idea what to do with.

"What thing in the morning?" Cash asked, sliding onto a stool next to me. I swear to God I could feel his heat, and I did my best to concentrate on his words.

"Um, just a thing at our shop. Nothing," I said.

Cash just raised an eyebrow at me. "You own a business?" he prompted.

I blew out a breath. Ah, well, it was fun while it lasted. This was typically the part where the men went running.

"Yes, I'm a psychic and I do tarot card readings and other services for my clientele. Luna offers healing potions and other home remedies on her side of the shop." I smiled brightly at him, waiting for the typical flash of fear or confusion.

"Far out," Cash said with a smile.

"Far out?" I echoed.

"Yeah, how neat. I'd love to learn more about it. Can I

take you to dinner tomorrow?" He leaned in, his eyes radiating his interest, his heat all but making me dizzy.

"You want to take me to dinner?" I asked, wondering if he'd just heard me correctly.

"Yes."

"You? Mr. Investor. Want to have dinner with the local psychic?" I asked again, wanting to make sure we were on the same page.

"And why wouldn't he?" Beau demanded, coming to stand in front of us, his hands on his hips.

"Yes, why wouldn't I?" Cash asked, turning to study me with curiosity.

"It's, um, it's just that not a lot of guys are fans of my talent," I said, whipping my finger in the air in a circular motion by my head.

"It doesn't bother me." Cash shrugged, casually dismissing it. I also shrugged my shoulders. If he didn't have a problem, then I wasn't going to make it a problem.

"Okay then," I said, watching his face.

"Great, it's a date! Can I pick you up at your place?" Cash asked and Beau rattled off my address before I could even respond.

"Wonderful. Looking forward to tomorrow, Althea," Cash said as he leaned in and brushed a kiss over my cheek before sauntering out.

"I...I..." I'd damn near lost my voice. Words were something that I was rarely without and I gaped at Beau. He hooted in laughter at the expression on my face.

"Told you I had a man for you, Althea Rose. Looks like you are getting a well-deserved treat. Served up on a yum-yum platter," Beau murmured, his eyes following Cash down the walkway.

"I can't believe this. I can't date guys like him! He looks like a model. Or something..." I began, totally flustered.

"Stop it this instant, Althea. Where is the badass woman that I've known my whole life? Who fights for her friends, says what's on her mind, and fills out a dress with every inch of her jaw-dropping curves? Hmm? Stop acting like a wilting flower and embrace it, girlfriend," Beau ordered.

"Yes, sir," I said meekly and slid from my stool, leaning over to hook my arm around his neck. "I love you."

"You too. Now don't come here for dinner tomorrow night or I'll be hanging on your every word. Make him take you someplace out of town. Or better yet, cook at your house."

Laughter bubbled up inside as I leaned back and met Beau's eyes.

"Oh shit. You don't cook. Order takeout. I'll drop it off."

"Stop. I'll get some appetizers. He can figure out dinner. Now, I have to go, I'm getting up at the crack of dawn to go diving with Trace."

"Hmmm," Beau trilled, moving a little away.

I snagged his arm.

"What was that?"

"Nothing. Looks like you have two hotties hanging on you," Beau said, a wicked glint in his eyes.

"Trace?" I said, genuinely shocked. Trace was just a

buddy of mine. We'd always had a platonic friendship centered on our love of diving.

"I see a love triangle shaping up," Beau called and waved me out, turning to help another customer.

Conversation over.

Which left only about a thousand questions darting through my head.

So much for sleep tonight, I thought, fighting to keep a silly grin off my face.

Chapter Five

MORNING CAME FAR TOO QUICKLY after a night of spotty sleep. I grumbled my way through the morning ritual Hank and I had established, almost burning my hand with hot coffee as I poured the liquid into a to-go container filled with ice. Dreams of Cash and Trace, and not necessarily apart, had kept me up and caused a blush to heat my face again this morning.

"It's been too long," I said out loud, knowing it was time for me to date again. It appeared I had been ignoring a few of the more basic needs in my life.

"Hank! New toy!" I called, pulling a new squeaky ball from my toy drawer. Hank's snorts echoed in the room as he raced across the floor and skidded to a halt at my feet. I sighed again, knowing that my wood floors would never be the same after having a dog, but one look at Hank's squishy face made me not give a damn.

"Ball!" I shouted and tossed the ball across the room, laughing as Hank went tumbling to scramble across the floor to retrieve it. Joyous squeaks greeted me and I smiled, knowing that would hold his interest for at least part of the day. I'd be back in a few hours to change after my dives and to let him out. Scanning the room for anything that I had missed, I grabbed the mesh bag filled with my dive gear and slipped the straps over my shoulders before stepping out onto the front porch. At just past 6:00 in the morning the light was low but the heat was already kicking in.

"There go my curls," I murmured, knowing my hair would poof out with the humidity. I hopped on my beach cruiser and pedaled my way down our street, turning left to follow a small bike path that would carry me directly to the wharf where Trace's dive boat was docked.

Scuba diving was in my blood. My parents had put a regulator in my mouth around the age of seven, and I'd never looked back. The absolute best way to start my day was 115 feet deep in water, taking pictures of turtles or whatever else crossed my path. Underwater photography had been a natural extension of my love of all things ocean, and I still surprised myself with how well my pictures sold. At first it had been a passion, but after people kept asking me for prints, I'd invested in some serious gear and now turned out some pretty phenomenal shots, if I do say so myself. Each year, my reputation grew and my two careers were now neck-and-neck for which brought in the most money.

Being a psychic certainly paid the bills, but I did it more out of habit than anything. I hadn't chosen to be a psychic; it had chosen me. Imagining life in a cubicle, though, was enough to make me forever grateful for the opportunities I did have. A wide smile lit my face as I wheeled my bike to the rack outside the entrance to the dock.

Here the wharf bustled with activity at this early hour. Between dive boats getting ready for their clients, to deep-sea fishing boats stocking their bait, making money from the ocean was a way of life in the Keys.

"Thea." A crew member of a threadbare fishing boat nodded at me and I waved at the crew as they lined up their poles in the holders that ranged along the back of the boat. I was a regular on these docks and continued to nod and wave at people as I walked down the floating planked dock until I reached Trace's smaller dive boat at the end. Painted white, with a neon red strip running along the hull, Trace's boat was leaner and faster than many of the larger scuba diving boats. Because of this, he kept his dive groups small and was able to take his clientele to some of the best places that were not overcrowded with larger groups of divers. Trace had gotten his nickname from his love of drawing, but it had followed him from art school to the Keys where he was also known to be one of the top search-and-rescue divers in the area. Whether looking for stranded boats or searching for missing persons, Trace's was always one of the first boats called after the Coast Guard. Oftentimes, he would even get to a stranded boat far before the Coast Guard could.

"Whooeee, look what the cat dragged in." An exaggerated southern drawl greeted me from the back of the boat and I laughed as I slipped my shoes off and stepped onto the gleaming white deck of the boat. At six foot two, Trace towered over me, all lean muscle and tattooed skin. His hair, bleached from the sun, was just long enough to pull back in a small nub at the base of his head. Shades covered what I knew to be deep blue eyes, and teeth flashed white in his face as he sized me up.

"Rough night?"

I blushed and looked away, moving to slide my dive bag onto the bench where Trace had already hooked up my buoyancy control device, or BCD in diver-speak, to a tank.

"I didn't sleep well," I said over my shoulder, forcing the thoughts of my naughty dreams from my mind. "Water will wake me up."

"Up for a current dive? The water along the south wall is prime and we're bound to see some larger stuff," Trace said, firing up the engines. I moved past him to where the front of the boat was tied and jumped on the dock to un-loop the rope from a hook. I held the rope as Trace reversed the boat, moving slowly so I could jump on the bow at the last minute.

"Current dive sounds great. You know I love the south wall."

"You'll want to take more wide-angle pictures then, no macro on this one," Trace observed and I nodded, knowing he was right. With this dive, we'd need to swim against the current for the first half of the dive before riding it back to the boat for the second half. It wouldn't leave much time or thought for up-close macro photography shots.

I pulled my camera from the bag and checked my gear, making sure everything was set just the way I liked it so I wouldn't have to make adjustments at 110 feet.

"You go out last night?" Trace called, directing the boat from the main canal, the houses of the rich passing slowly by us.

"Just to Lucky's for one with Luna," I said, pulling my t-shirt over my head and shimmying out of my shorts. I wore a fairly skimpy bikini underneath, not something that I would usually lounge on the beach with, but it was easy to slip a wetsuit over. I bent over to pull my wetsuit out of the bag and, straightening, I caught Trace's eye.

"What?" I said.

"Nothing, I like that suit on you," he said, turning back to the wheel to pump the speed up a bit as we left the channel.

He liked this suit on me? I'd worn this suit easily fifty times around him. Why the compliment now? Dying to take a peek in his brain, but my ethics preventing me from doing so, I smiled at him instead.

"Thanks, $19.99 on sale from Target."

"It does nice things for your curves."

Again, he looked at me, holding my gaze longer than usual. I wished I could see behind his glasses to his eyes, wondering desperately what game we were playing here.

"Well, my curves have a mind of their own," I said lamely and bent again to hide the blush on my face as I stepped into my thin skin wetsuit and pulled it up, shimmying into the suit, knowing all of my bits were bouncing about as I pulled it up to my waist and let it hang loose. It was too hot to zip all the way into the suit until we were close to getting in the water.

Trace and I had been friends since he first moved to the Keys about six years ago. The girls of the town had flocked to his easy-going surfer vibe and he'd won over more than one girl by offering to draw her.

Sans clothes, naturally.

Diving had brought us together, but a shared sense of humor and an honest look at the trials of dating in a small town had cemented our friendship. My anxiety kicked up a notch as I wondered if there would be a shift in the foundation that I took for granted in our relationship.

"You going to tell me about your hot date or not?" Trace said easily, but my back stiffened at the hint of ice under his words.

"Word travels fast," I observed, unaccountably angry. Why should I be? I'd lived in Tequila Key my whole life. You couldn't so much as order something from Amazon without the whole neighborhood watching the delivery driver come down the road. A hot new investor in town? I'd be crazy to think something like that would be kept under wraps. Surely half of the rich daughters in Port Atticus were pulling out their pearls and push-up bras in order to catch Cash's eye.

"Like that's a surprise?" Trace asked. "Buoy," he said, pointing to the front of the boat. I was grateful for the distraction. Moving to the bow of the boat, I picked up a long pole with a hook to catch the buoy line to attach the boat to. Permanent anchors had been dropped all over the coastline for dive boats to easily hook up to, thus ensuring that the coral wouldn't be constantly damaged by anchors being dropped daily.

I didn't know what to say to the anger in Trace's voice. We'd always been able to tell each other about our various love interests and there had never been a problem before. But for the first time in years, we were both single at the same time. I wondered if he was jealous that I had a date and he didn't. Men had a tendency to get a little ornery when they went too long without some loving. Unlike us mature women, I thought with a mild snort and moved to check that the air in my tank was on.

"So? Where are you going?" Trace insisted on continuing the conversation, coming to stand next to me as he turned the air on for his tank.

"I don't know. He's picking me up at seven. Is that okay with you, boss?" I asked cheekily, slipping my arms into my dive suit and turning for him to zip up the back. I gasped as he yanked me closer than necessary and slowly zipped my wetsuit up.

"Watch yourself, Althea," Trace said, his voice at my ear, his breath hot on my neck. Damn if tingles of excitement didn't race down my back and skitter into my stomach in a pool of lust as he held me a second too long, pressed back against his body.

I stepped shakily away and then turned to help him zip his suit up, my eyes tracing up the muscles of his tanned back, following the line of tattoos up his arms. Finishing quickly, I stepped back and sat on the bench, sliding my BCD on over my shoulders and snapping the belt on my waist closed. Trace mirrored my motions and we both stood awkwardly under the weight of our tanks and faced each other, running our hands over each other's regulators and weight belts, doing a final safety check before we began our dive.

"Do you have a problem with Cash?" I blurted out as we stood at the back of the boat, ready to do a giant stride into the water.

Trace turned and met my eyes through his mask.

"I have no problem with him. My problem is with you

going on a date with him and not me," he said before putting a regulator in his mouth and striding into the water. My mouth dropped as panic mixed with lust punched my stomach. Trace bobbed for a moment at the surface, signaling to me that he was okay.

"It's not like you've asked me!" I shouted at him, angry that he had sprung this on me now, angry that he thought he could suddenly step into my life and muck things up for me. I slammed my regulator into my mouth and holding my mask with one arm, my camera with the other, I launched myself into the water.

There's nothing quite like jumping off a boat into clear blue water to see unimaginable strength and delicate beauty just waiting to be discovered beneath the surface. It is an entirely different world, one where we are the observers, invited to watch the intricate dance of nature play out before us.

I flashed an okay sign to Trace before beginning my descent to the floor below. Bubbles scattered past my face as I floated gently down to the bottom, bumping a little extra air into my BCD to neutralize my buoyancy. Together, Trace and I met at the bottom and he motioned towards a tunnel through the coral that would lead us out over the drop-off. A shot of adrenalin, far better than a morning cup of coffee, raced through me as I followed him through the coral tunnel, pulling my regulators close to keep from getting caught on the coral, and inching my way along until we both emerged, slightly giddy, to float over the wall.

Trace immediately motioned to me to get moving and I remembered that he had said there was a current today. We

turned to face it and began to swim, moving together naturally, totally in synch with each other. I snapped some
pictures as I kicked against the current, stealing glances
down at the 4,000-foot drop-off that loomed below me – a
deep blue abyss. There was nothing like looking straight
into the depths of the ocean to put some perspective on
your smallness in this universe, I thought.

The sound of clanging on a tank caused me to shoot
my head up and I looked to where Trace pointed.

A trio of eagle rays, so perfectly fluid they looked like
they were flying, moved delicately through the water in
front of us. I brought my camera up and took shot after
shot as my heart sang, looking at their beauty and grace. I
could imagine a symphony or some glorious music playing
in the background as they sliced their way through the
water, so sure of their place in the ocean.

I turned back to Trace and he brought his hands to his
face, mimicking a bravo kiss. I smiled, knowing that in
that moment, we were back on track.

The rest of the dive passed in a blur of giddiness, as I
rode the current back to the boat with Trace, all but
laughing into my regulator as we flew past the wall and
startled a turtle with our movements. Hating that the dive
had to be over, I kicked in lazy circles at our fifteen-foot
safety stop, hoping that the weirdness of this morning
would pass and that Trace and I would be back on even
ground. I just couldn't see myself dating one of my best
friends. Ultimately, our friendship was too high a price to
pay for love, I decided as I held the step ladder at the back
of the boat and slid my fins off my feet, chucking each one
onto the boat before pulling myself up and waddling over

to sit on the bench, sliding my tank into the holder behind me.

Trace surfaced and pulled himself easily from the water, his smile saying it all.

"Those rays!" I exclaimed, a smile lighting my face.

"Biggest ones I've seen in months!" Trace said back, smiling at me as he sat to unbuckle his BCD.

I blew out a breath in relief as I stood and stripped off my wetsuit, snagging a towel to wrap around me quickly. I didn't want the subject of my curves to come up again.

"I can't wait to go through my pictures. I already know one client who has been asking for eagle rays specifically. The trio will be perfect for a nice piece over a sofa," I gushed as I sank my camera into the freshwater bin on the floor to rinse it of the salt water.

"We doing another?" Trace asked, nodding towards the water.

"What time is it?" I asked. We'd need at least an hour of surface time before another dive. I wasn't sure if I wanted to spend an hour with Trace after the weirdness of this morning. Too much going on for me to get my head mired in that today, I thought, as I pushed his comment about going on a date with him from my head.

"Almost nine."

"Let's call it. I have an earlier client today," I said, not meeting his eyes. And, I needed to run around my house to do a rush clean and pick an outfit for tonight, all before I left for the shop.

"Fine," Trace said shortly, moving to the front of the boat to unhook the buoy. Man, was he cranky today.

"Yup, another glorious day of channeling dead cats

and telling people that I won't give them the winning lottery numbers," I said dryly, unwrapping a granola bar as Trace moved to the wheel of the boat and started the engine.

Trace snorted a laugh and I felt the tension ease again.

"I'm really annoyed that you haven't given *me* the winning lotto numbers yet," he said and I laughed, loving that he didn't think twice about what I did for a living.

"Ah well, you know, trade secrets and all that."

Trace laughed and then his face got serious again.

"Well, have fun with Mr. Fancy Investor tonight," he said, his eyes on the water ahead of him as we motored into the channel towards the docks.

"Do you have a problem with him?" I asked for the second time, tilting my head at Trace as I tied my soggy curls in a knot on top of my head.

"I don't like him," Trace said simply.

"Well, what the hell does that mean? I didn't know you knew him," I said, exasperation lacing my voice.

"I've met him. I don't like him." Trace shrugged a shoulder and didn't say anything else. A part of me wondered if it was because of how good-looking Cash was. Trace was used to being one of the few hot – and available – men in Tequila Key. Deciding it had to be something like that, and not anything more sinister, I shrugged.

"Well, I guess I'll let you know what I think after I have dinner with him," I said lightly, wanting the subject matter to be closed. I was annoyed that this was even an issue. For the first time in ages, I had a decidedly delicious dating prospect and Trace wanted to rain on my parade.

Forget it, I thought as we approached our dock and Trace slowed the boat.

I moved to the top of the boat and jumped onto the dock with the line in my hand, my movements practiced.

Deciding not to stay and chat like I usually did, I hopped onto the boat and grabbed my bag, slipping the straps over my shoulders and sliding my feet into my sandals.

"Thanks, this was fun. Add it to my tab," I said with a smile, knowing that Trace wouldn't charge me for the air as it was just as fun for him to dive without clients as it was for me to go to take pictures.

"Have fun tonight," Trace said dryly, his eyes again hidden behind his sunglasses.

"Thanks," I said, moving down the dock. Turning, I looked back at him, standing in just his swimsuit, watching me walk away. Damn, but he was hot.

"We on for Friday?" I asked, our routine being typically a Wednesday and Friday dive each week.

"Can't, have a full boat. Saturday?"

"Done," I said, moving away before any other uncomfortable topic could come up. There were clients to be read, dresses to be picked out, and dogs to be played with. I couldn't spend time worrying about Trace's little funk this morning.

I had bigger fish to fry today.

Chapter Six

A FANCY CAR was parked outside our shop when I arrived later that morning. As I drew closer, I could see that it was an Audi done up in a white exterior with cream interior detailing. Shamelessly, I scanned the car with my mind to prepare myself and groaned.

Debating whether to turn around and go back home for another hour, I sighed as I saw Luna at the front window of her shop, raising an arm to greet me.

"Busted," I said, getting off my bike and wheeling it to the front where I locked it to the rack.

I'd had time to shower and gel my hair – in a vain attempt to keep my curls under control – throw on another cute maxi, lay out a bright red dress for dinner, and clean the house of any embarrassing articles before I biked into the store, still about a half hour early for my first appointment. I'd had a mind to talk to Luna about how weird Trace had been this morning, but now it looked like I'd be stuck with our client.

I pushed the door open, savoring the cool wash of air

on my warm skin before I pasted a bright smile on my face.

"Morning!" I said, turning to Luna and our client.

Mrs. Janelle Whittier was about fifteen years younger than her husband, Theodore, and I still wasn't quite sure how he had managed to marry her. Perfectly cropped blonde hair, a white sweater tied over her polka-dotted dress, and dripping in pearls, she was the antithesis of everything I loved about this town.

"Janelle, lovely to see you again," I said.

"Althea, I haven't seen you in ages," she trilled, coming over to air kiss me on each cheek. "I wanted to stop by your cute shop to see if I could find any gifts for my sister's birthday but…it's not quite to my taste," she said, an eyebrow raised in disapproval at the row of crystals on the table next to me.

"Really? I'm quite certain your sister would love these hand-made soaps and bath salts," I said, steering her towards a table full of luscious soaps wrapped in hand-dyed paper.

"Oh, I hadn't seen these. Well, yes, I suppose those would work," she said, running her hands over her pearls, and not picking up any of the soaps. That's when I knew she'd really come to see me.

"Did you need anything else?" I asked chirpily.

"Well, yes, I suppose, a reading would be nice. I'll just get set up next door," she said, trailing past the screen into my side of the shop where Luna had already turned my lamps on. My mouth dropped open at the audacity of Janelle's actions. I turned and widened my eyes at Luna, who just held up her hands helplessly. The nerve of this woman! She hadn't even asked if I had an appointment scheduled.

"Um, Janelle, I have an appointment at eleven," I said, glancing at my watch as I cursed softly under my breath and moved across the room, pulling the screen shut behind me.

"That's fine, plenty of time," Janelle said, sliding into my client's seat, her back ramrod straight. She sniffed as she looked around my room, her eyes landing on my skeleton in the corner. I could all but feel the palpable waves of disgust coming off of her.

Moving to my table, I sat in my chair, and looked across at her. Instead of grabbing my cards right away, I needed to be clear.

"A half hour reading is $100," I said, upping the price slightly because of my annoyance.

"That's fine. Can we start?" Janelle shifted in her chair, eyeing me closely.

"Because of the brevity of the reading I'll ask if you are interested in a general outlook or if you have specific questions that you would like answered." It wasn't a typical move for me but I sensed there was a mission behind Miss Country Club's arrival at my doorstep.

"Direct question," she decided.

I handed her my tarot cards.

"Shuffle as many times as you'd like and then cut the deck in three, please," I said, allowing my shields to drop so I could tune in to that part of my brain that allowed me to catch glimpses into the future. A dark sense of foreboding crept out of the shadows of my mind and it was all I could do not to gasp. Something was very wrong.

"Is this confidential?" Janelle asked, her fingers running over her pearls.

"Always. I wouldn't be in business if it wasn't," I said.

"Okay, my first question is…" her eyes darted around the room before she lowered her face, all but whispering into the table, "should I leave Theo?"

Thank God for years in training on schooling my facial expressions, as I didn't react in the slightest. I picked up the cards and began to deal, laying out a Celtic Cross formation.

"What is that?"

"This is a Celtic Cross. Each card holds different meanings towards the question you've asked, for example, this card tells you how you feel about the situation…" I began but she waved her hand in the air, cutting me off.

"I don't care. Yes or no?"

I stopped – shocked that she wanted such a blunt answer.

"You have to understand there is no absolute right answer. Even if I tell you one answer, you still have free will to do as you wish. The best that I can tell you is if a situation will work out favorably if you make that decision," I said cautiously, needing her to understand that our choices always held weight and that destiny was a fickle mistress.

Janelle sighed and rolled her eyes.

"Fine, just tell me if I'll be okay if I leave Theo," she said, annoyance lacing her voice.

I read through the cards again and then closed my eyes. The cards were telling me that she shouldn't leave him. But I also could tell that she didn't want to hear that answer. In situations like this, I always deferred to the cards.

"This particular layout is suggesting that you might be happier if you stay with Theo," I said gently, and saw anger flash across Janelle's face.

"You would say that," she spit out, pushing back from the table.

"Excuse me? I didn't pull the cards, you did," I pointed out.

"It's because you don't want me to go out with Cash," Janelle spit at me, effectively causing me to shut up as I tried to register her words.

"Cash?" I said stupidly, trying to understand where she was going with this.

"Cash, the man with whom you have a date this evening. The man who cancelled plans with me to be with you." Janelle leaned over, her hand gripping the purple velvet of my tablecloth so tightly that I feared she would rip the whole thing off. I placed my hands on the table, ready to catch my crystal ball if it went flying.

"I have no idea what this has to do with Cash, but I suggest you get the hell out of my shop," I said easily, meeting her eyes.

"You think that just because you are some tattooed tart with big boobs that you can attract a man like Cash, but money talks, Althea. Cash will return to his like soon enough," she said, a smirk crossing her face as she straightened, smoothing her dress with manicured hands.

"I'm sorry, but aren't you currently married? Threaten me again and I'll be happy to tell Theo about this little conversation," I said heatedly.

A wave of fear hit me so badly that my stomach curdled and I gulped against the nausea that gripped me. A bright sheen of tears had jumped into Janelle's eyes and she'd brought her hand to her face.

"You promised you wouldn't say anything," she exclaimed.

"Well, don't come in here attacking me," I said, exasperated. "God, you think you can just walk all over everyone. Hasn't anyone taught you manners? Or kindness? Get out of my shop. What I do with Cash, or anyone else, is my own damn business. Oh, reading's free of charge," I said scathingly as she stormed from my shop, the bells on the door tinkling way too cheerfully for the enraged woman that stalked beneath them.

In seconds, Luna stepped into my room, a smudge stick lit in her hand, as she walked around the room banishing the bad energy.

"What the hell was that about?" Luna whispered, darting a glance my way.

"I have no idea. But it seems to me the Whittiers don't have the perfect life they are trying to make it out to be," I said, shaking my head, trying to dispel that weird rush of fear that had hit me. Must have been because Mrs. Perfect didn't want to lose her status in this town. "She wants to leave him."

Luna stopped smudging and shot me a glance over her shoulder.

"That's so strange to me. He's besotted with her."

"He is?" I said, wondering how Luna knew that. The only thing I had seen Theodore besotted with was his wallet.

"He is. He lights up when she's around. And you should see him when he plays catch with his boy. I know you don't like Theodore, but he's not all bad."

"I guess...I just don't know that side of him," I said, wondering how often Luna saw Theodore with his son.

"I couldn't help but listen in...did Janelle say she had plans with Cash?" Luna asked, her perfectly arched eyebrow raised in concern.

Biting my bottom lip, I nodded, unsure how to respond.

"There has to be an explanation. Cash doesn't strike me as the type to try to date a married woman," Luna said.

"How do you know? We don't even know him," I pointed out, cranky at the prospect that my super-hot date was turning out to be something that I shouldn't touch with a ten-foot pole.

"Nothing is as it seems," Luna remarked, "and, I trust Beau. If he wants to work with Cash, then I have to think Cash is a good man," she said, carrying her smudge stick with her to her shop. I sighed and smoothed my tablecloth back out, pulling out a different pack of tarot cards for my next client. I'd need to clear the energy from the first deck later. My bells chimed and I looked up and smiled.

"Mrs. Matthews, so nice to see you," I said.

"Now, dear, I hear you can speak to our pets that have passed on."

Chapter Seven

HOURS LATER, I was kicked back with an iced tea and a chicken salad sandwich from Luca's Deli – I had to eat there while I still could – when I heard a customer come in to Luna's side of the store. A fluttery laugh reached me and I realized it was Luna's flirty laugh. I leaned a bit to peek my head around the screen.

Miami club guy!

I ducked my head back, knowing that Luna would want some privacy with him since she thought he was so cute, and turned up my music a bit more to cover their voices. Shaking my head, I began the process of clearing energy from the tarot deck that Janelle had used, idly wondering why Luna thought Miami club guy was so cute.

He was too slick for me. His perfectly creased pants made me nervous. I'd never be able to date a guy that was more put together than me, I thought.

So why was I going out with Cash? I asked myself as I shuffled the deck, allowing the negative energy to seep away from the cards.

Because he's a dead ringer for Channing Tatum and I'm dying to see if he can dance like the guys in *Magic Mike* do, my baser self whispered to me and I snorted.

Idly, I eyed my scrying ball and wondered if I really needed Luna's seeing spell to dip into the future. Since I had more power than her in that area, typically I just needed to get in my zone and ask my spirit guides for a little help with clearing the clouds from my vision. The foreboding had yet to leave my mind and I suspected that it wasn't going to leave until I did something about it. Not wanting to deal with Luna's temper if I went ahead and did the spell on my own, I sighed and pushed my scrying ball away. Turning my right arm up, I looked at the inside of my arm and wondered what tattoo I should add when a knock on my screen caused me to jump.

"Ahem, yes?"

Luna poked her head around the screen and smiled at me, her cheeks flush with a light pink color.

"Renaldo would like to know if he could have a reading with you. I wasn't sure if you had blocked off time for walk-ins today," she said, raising her eyebrows at me in question.

"Renaldo?" I said, raising an eyebrow at her already familiar use of Miami club guy's name.

"Erm, yes," she said, smiling sheepishly at me.

I sighed and pulled out a different stack of cards, waving at Luna in a go-ahead motion.

Luna pushed the screen back and motioned for Renaldo to come into my room. I didn't rise to greet him, instead staying seated as I scanned him, giving him a healthy dose of warning in my look. I didn't trust him already, and here he was sniffing around my best friend.

"Hello, so many thanks for you to meet with me," Renaldo said, putting his hand out. Today he wore a white silk shirt that set off his tan skin. A glint of gold at his neck reminded me of the cross he wore. Sniffing, I looked at his trousers.

Perfect pleats.

I shook his hand, allowing my walls to go down so I could let impressions flood me. His dark brown eyes stayed on mine as I motioned for him to sit. Oddly, fear rose to the top of the emotions I was reading from him.

Luna hovered at the door, looking anxiously between the both of us.

"Thanks, Luna. We'll come out when we are done," I said, smiling tightly at her. She jumped a little and then nodded, pulling the screen back and returning to the cool white of her room.

"So, Renaldo, you're from Puerto Rico, yes?" I asked, having pulled that tid-bit from his mind, shuffling the cards as I eyed him.

"Yes, ma'am," he said automatically.

I rolled my eyes and shook my head at him.

"Call me Althea, please. Ma'am is for my mother."

"Althea, yes, I am from Puerto Rico."

"You're Catholic?" I asked, pointing to the cross at his neck.

"Yes, I am Catholic."

"So why are you here then? Don't you go to church and ask for guidance?" I asked, knowing that the sarcasm was strong with me today. I don't know what it was about this guy, but he just rubbed me the wrong way.

"Please, understand that God works in mysterious ways. You can find answers in many areas," Renaldo said, shrugging his shoulders casually and dismissing centuries of judgment on my profession by the Catholic Church.

"Okay then," I said, deciding it wasn't the best time to get into an argument about this. I wasn't religious by any means, but I was spiritual to a fault. Perhaps it was because my gift gave me a greater peek into the unknown that so many people were seeking to understand and therefore I was quite solid on where I stood spiritually.

"So, Renaldo, what are you in town for?" I asked as I put my deck of tarot cards down on the purple velvet in front of me.

"I'm working with a group of investors and the City Council, like Mr. Whittier, on helping to develop a few properties," he said simply.

"And your role specifically is...?" I asked, raising an eyebrow at him.

"I was understood that the questions were for me to be asking," he said, smiling lightly at me, his eyes hard with warning.

"Okay then," I said, pushing the cards across to him. "Shuffle the cards and then cut them in three stacks. Think of the question you want answered while you shuffle."

I watched Renaldo as he shuffled, reaching out again to get a read on him with my mind. A gray cloud of fear seemed to cling to his shoulders, and I couldn't get past it to see what was causing it. A glimpse of a seaplane came through, as well as a large barrel floating on the water. I had no idea what this could possibly mean and I snapped back to attention when he split the cards in front of me.

"Your question?" I asked, lifting my eyes to meet his.

He stared at me, his eyes dark with fear, as he whispered, "Should I stay on this job?"

It wasn't an unusual question to ask a psychic; it was just that the fear in his eyes was creeping me out.

I pulled cards from the middle pile, laying them out in a Celtic Cross formation again. As I turned each card over, dread began to form.

I flipped over the last card, the outcome card, and my hand stilled on the face of it, trepidation lacing my spine, as I didn't want to lift my fingers and reveal the card to him.

"Show me the card," he whispered.

I swallowed as I lifted my hand from the card, watching his face carefully.

Death.

The word etched beneath the depiction of a skeleton holding a black flag, riding a white horse, conveyed the message without me having to say it.

Renaldo's eyes widened and he leaned back in his chair, crossing his arms over his chest as if to protect himself.

"Now," I said, raising my hand in caution, "the death card does not mean you will die. It can also signal ending a contract, time for a change, or moving on. My read of this card would be that, yes, it might be in your best interest to leave this job and return home," I said, trying to soothe the waves of fear that I felt emanating from him.

Liar, my brain whispered to me.

And I knew it to be true, I thought. In my entire time reading tarot, I had never had the death card literally mean the death of a client that sat before me. And yet, I sat there, watching Renaldo, and knew that he was a dead man walking.

I just didn't know why.

"You're quite certain I should leave?" Renaldo asked again.

I bit my tongue and nodded, not knowing what else to say.

He nodded once and stood, reaching into his back pocket and dropping a couple of hundred-dollar bills on my table.

"Wait, do you have any more questions? That's too much money for one question," I protested.

"Keep it. Thank you for being honest with me," he said and nodded once more before ducking behind the screen.

Guilt kicked up my spine as I looked down at the money. I hadn't been totally honest with him, had I? I'd told him to leave, hadn't I? But my instincts said that something with his job would cause his death. Straining my mind, I tried to see if there was a work-related accident I could warn him about – then I stilled, remembering my mother's words.

Do not try to change someone's fate. Their choices have led them there.

It wasn't always easy being a psychic. You were privy to people's hopes, their dreams, their sadness, their greed…the list went on and on. For the most part, my job was pretty cool, but readings like today's made me question whether I should hang it all up and only be an underwater photographer. I couldn't imagine how hard it was to be a doctor who had to deliver bad news. In retrospect, maybe my job wasn't as bad as theirs was. Thoughts swirled around my brain, tumbling on top of each other as anxiety kicked up my back.

"He's cute, huh?"

Luna's voice cut into my reprieve and I jerked my head up, pasting a smile on my face.

"If you're into that type," I said.

"Well, I most certainly am. He asked me to dinner tonight, which means I've got to close up if I want to get ready," Luna trilled as she ducked out of my room and I heard her walking around her shop, turning off lights. Dread filled my heart and I wanted to say something to her, to let her know not to get her hopes up, but I couldn't break confidentiality.

Being a psychic sucked sometimes.

Chapter Eight

AN HOUR LATER, I threw the ball while sitting on the back porch, and sipped a glass of wine to soothe my nerves. The reading with Renaldo was still on my mind and anxiety about seeing Cash again kicked through my stomach.

Hank barked at me.

"Oh? I didn't toss the ball fast enough for you?" I said, leaning down to gingerly pick up the soggy ball, doing my best to keep my date-night outfit from getting dirty.

I'd gone with red. Screaming, siren red that highlighted the duskiness of my skin tone and clashed nicely with my pink hair. The neck scooped low enough to entice, but not enough to proclaim that an invitation inside would happen after dinner. With cap sleeves and a peplum top, the dress highlighted the things that I wanted to show off and hid the parts that I preferred to be hidden. It was a win-win in my book. I'd left my curly hair to tumble down my back, clipping each side back with a comb. Large silver hoops and nude strappy sandals completed my outfit and I desperately hoped that I wasn't overdressed.

A knock at the door sent Hank into a frenzy of barking and I almost dumped my wine down my lap.

"Bring it down a notch," I whispered to myself and stood up, smoothing my dress before walking through my kitchen, past where I had hastily prepared some appetizers, to the front door.

"Hank, sit," I said to the dog and he sat, his black-and-white body quivering with energy as he waited to see who was behind the door. Unlocking my deadbolt, I eased the door open to find Cash, dressed in linen pants and shirt, clutching a bouquet of sunflowers on my porch.

I swear to all that is holy, this man is too good-looking to be for real, I thought as my mouth went dry.

"Hi," I said, easing the door open and immediately turning to Hank. "Hank, guest. Nice manners," I ordered and Hank stood, pressing his nose into Cash's pants, a peculiar habit that Bostons have when they meet someone. Judging him not to be the enemy, Hank turned and raced across the room to find a toy to present to Cash.

"That's Hank," I said with a smile, opening the door wider. "Come in, please."

"Can I just say wow," he said and I turned to look at the explosion of color that rocketed across my living room.

"Oh, I know, there's a lot going on here," I said, waving my hand at the walls before turning to look at him and realizing that he wasn't looking at the walls.

His eyes were trained on my dress.

"Oh," I said, breathing slowly.

"You look wonderful," Cash said and held out the flowers to me.

"Thank you," I said, hiding my smile in the petals as I sniffed the flowers, turning to walk towards the kitchen to find a vase. "Make yourself at home, I'm just going to find a vase. Do you prefer wine or beer?"

"I'll take a beer if you have it," he called, stopping to admire a blown-up print of a Queen angelfish that I had tucked over my couch.

"Corona okay?"

"Perfect."

Hank had now brought three of his most favorite toys to Cash, dropping them at his feet and cocking his head, waiting for a response. I heard the ball bounce across the floor as I dug in the cupboard for my favorite cobalt blue vase for the sunflowers. Cash had picked up on the hint.

After filling the vase with flowers, I paused to admire my work, trying not to mentally squeal over Cash having brought me flowers. I'd swoon later, in private, like the dignified woman that I am.

"How very Van Gogh of you," Cash said, gesturing to the flowers.

I tilted my head at it and laughed, realizing that I had unintentionally recreated the famous painting.

"Beer," I said, handing the Corona to him and moving back to the fridge. "Lime?" I'd cut some earlier, thinking he would probably drink beer.

"Sure, thanks. This is a great place," Cash said.

"Thanks, I love it. I know it's a little crazy, but it's just...me," I said simply, snagging the tray of cheese and meats that I had prepared earlier.

"Want to sit on the porch or too hot for you?"

"Porch is fine; here, let me help," Cash said, reaching for the tray, his arm brushing across mine and sending heat trailing up my body.

Whoo, boy, did I need to calm down, I thought.

We moved onto the porch and I clicked on the large plantation fans so they swirled lazily above us, moving the hot air and giving some reprieve to the stickiness. Hank panted on the grass, taking a break from ball chasing to cool down.

"Is that the beach?" Cash asked, straining to see my secret spot.

"Yup, it's the best part of this house. You can't even tell from the front."

"No kidding, this is an amazing spot," he said, settling into the chair and crossing his foot over his knee. He turned to look at me and I felt that low tug of lust again. I sighed, shaking my head a bit.

"What?"

"You're just too ridiculously good-looking," I laughed, surprised at myself.

"Thanks, I think?" he said, cracking a smile that I'm sure would have thousands of women falling at his feet.

"That smile must help you in negotiations," I said, raising an eyebrow at him, and he laughed.

"It doesn't hurt. You're not so bad yourself, Ms. Althea. I saw you enter the tiki bar the other night and couldn't take my eyes off of you."

I blushed but couldn't help smiling. Damn, if this man had this much game, I was toast.

"Thanks, everyone says that," I said cheekily, tossing

my hair over my shoulder but giving him a smile to let him know I was joking. He laughed at me and raised his glass to clink against mine.

"I look forward to getting to know you better. Maybe you can fill me in on the town a bit," Cash said, leaning over to pop a cube of cheese into his mouth. I had to draw my eyes away from his lips.

"Well, it's a small town in its own right...are you really moving down here?" I said, raising an eyebrow at him.

"I am."

"From where?"

"Boston."

"Boston? Won't you find this to be a bit of a slower pace?" I asked incredulously.

"Yes, but the cold gets annoying after a while. There's so much beauty here. And...there's money to be made," Cash said.

"I suppose. I'd love to learn more about what you are working on here, aside from Beau's new restaurant — which I am over the moon about, by the way."

"He's great," Cash said, further working his way into my heart by complimenting my best friend.

"I know. There's so much good in him...ugh, I just love him," I gushed.

"I suspect the restaurant's going to be a huge hit."

"We certainly could use some more upscale dining," I agreed. "Speaking of...where are we going to dinner?"

"The next Key over. A nice little restaurant on the water," Cash said easily. For some reason, the thought of leaving town made me flash back to Janelle's angry face earlier today. Did he want to take me to dinner out of town so people wouldn't know that we had gone on a date? Wondering if he was lining up dates with women all over the place, I nibbled at my lip.

"Something wrong with that? I figured you'd like a change of pace," Cash said, raising an eyebrow at me.

"No, that's fine. Probably for the best, you know, small towns love to gossip. Pretty much everyone knows everyone else's business here," I said lightly, hoping he could read the underlying warning in my voice.

"Yes, that will take some getting used to," Cash agreed and finished his beer.

"Would you like another?"

"We should get going, our reservations are in a half hour. Do you want help cleaning up?" Cash asked, the consummate gentleman.

"Please, I need to get Hank in and feed him," I said, turning to call for Hank. "Hank, you hungry?"

Hank raced up the yard and barreled past us to dance in front of his dish.

We both laughed and I shook my earlier concerns off of my shoulders. I was a psychic, wasn't I? It would be hard to pull something over on me. There was no reason for me to be worried. Determined to let myself enjoy a nice dinner with a handsome man without looking for ulterior motives, I shrugged off my concerns and moved to Cash, leaning up to kiss him on the cheek.

"What was that for?" he asked, a look of pleasant surprise crossing his face. His hands automatically came to rest at my waist and a shiver raced through me at his touch.

"Thanks for the flowers," I said sweetly and moved

from his grasp, hearing a muffled groan behind me. I bit down on a laugh and turned to him.

"Alright, cutie, show me your fancy dinner place."

"My pleasure," Cash said, excitement lighting up his face.

Well, if this was going to end badly, my spidey senses weren't tingling.

And so help me, even if it was – I was all in.

Chapter Nine

"A CRAB SHACK?" I said, laughing as we pulled up to a quaint-looking shack tucked just off the highway on a long stretch of rocky beach.

"You haven't been here? I'm surprised," Cash said, coming around to open my door. He drove a new four-door Jeep Wrangler in white, and seeing him at the wheel had prompted a vivid fantasy of us camping together.

Without our clothes.

"I...I haven't," I said, smiling up at him as he took my hand to pull me from the car. Our bodies brushed and I just wanted to lean in and take a little nip at his throat, but instead I moved past him, pretending to be unaffected.

"It's great. This is my second time here. Though it looks fairly casual from the outside, the interior is really nice," Cash said, taking my hand and helping me down a flagstone path.

"Good, I was about to say...I'm probably overdressed," I said lightly, concentrating on not catching my wedge heels on the stones and trying not to get overly excited about holding Cash's hand.

"Nah, you'll be fine," Cash said and stopped to hold the door open for me, letting out the scent of butter and garlic.

"Mmm, smells amazing," I said as I stepped into a surprisingly charming dining room. Tables with gray linen cloths were clustered together and fat candles sputtered in the middle of each. Black-and-white photos of the ocean were printed and framed with driftwood on the walls.

"This is great," I said, turning to smile at Cash.

"Isn't it?" He nodded to the hostess. "Table for Williams."

"Yes, sir, just this way," the young blonde said, flipping her hair back and motioning for us to squeeze through the tables until we reached a spot right by the window.

"This is great," I repeated as I sat, placing the napkin on my lap and turning to look out to where the sun was beginning to dip into the horizon. A breeze tickled my nose and the lilting sound of steel drums could be heard over the patrons' chatter.

"They don't just have crab...I may get the lobster too," Cash said, smiling at me, and my heart skipped a beat just looking at his face. He seemed so happy, so at ease with who he was, it was like a low hum of power and sexuality vibrated from him.

"I'm down for crab," I said easily, flipping my menu closed.

"Do you drink?"

"I do, yes, but rarely heavily," I said, smiling at him.

"Ah, I wasn't sure if it, uh, affected things," he said, pointing to my head.

I tilted my head at him, confused, before realizing he was referencing my psychic gift.

"Oh! Yes, if I have more than two or three drinks, I won't see clients in the morning because a hangover could cloud any visions I might get," I said, stopping as our waitress approached and rattled off the dinner specials.

"We'll have a bottle of the Chablis," Cash said to her, turning to raise an eyebrow in question at me. I nodded my acceptance and I was secretly thrilled at having a man order for me. I wouldn't like it all the time, but I liked knowing he was willing to take control and make decisions too.

Perhaps I'd dated too many wimpy men in my life, I mused.

"So, before we were interrupted, you were saying that you won't drink much if you have clients," Cash said, smiling as the waitress came back with a bottle in an ice bucket and two glasses. I was pleased to see a steaming basket of cornbread accompanied the wine.

"I don't. I try to be the best at what I do and I don't think it's fair to give a reading if I'm not clear-headed. That goes for if I'm sick too," I said, nodding when Cash held up the breadbasket. Reaching in, I snagged a chunk of bread and broke it into two pieces on my plate.

"That's ethical," Cash agreed.

"Yeah, you wouldn't think it, but psychics have a code of ethics just like every other business," I said as I spread butter on my bread. Taking a bite, I groaned as the bread all but melted in my mouth.

"Good?" Cash laughed.

"So good. I can tell this place is going to be great already," I said.

"What other rules do you abide by in your business?"

"Well, for one, you don't mess with someone's fate," I said, reaching for my glass of wine.

"How so?"

I shrugged, allowing the sweet liquid to cool my throat before continuing.

"You can't sugar coat stuff for people or tell them what they want to hear. For one, it's not good business. Even if in the moment it would make the client happy, down the road they'll realize that you were lying when things don't go the way they wanted and they'll never come back to you."

"So you base your business on being honest, which in turn gives you good word-of-mouth," Cash said.

"I do," I said and felt guilt creeping up my throat as I flashed back to Renaldo's reading earlier that day. "Hey, um, how do you know Renaldo?"

"Renaldo? He's working with a group of investors we are courting to finish funding a few properties. There are some potential condo developments out past Port Atticus."

"Hmm," I said.

"Why?"

"Cash, great to see you again," a voice boomed out, interrupting our conversation and causing me to jump in my seat. I groaned as I saw Theodore Whittier pushing his way through the tables, his ruddy face glowing with a thin sheen of sweat.

"Theodore," Cash said and then when Theodore didn't

look at me, he put his hand out towards me. "And I'm sure you know my date, Althea Rose."

Theodore bristled and turned, giving me a curt nod. "Althea."

"Theodore, just a real pleasure to see you again," I said, allowing sarcasm to slip into my voice.

Theodore sniffed.

"So this is who you cancelled our evening plans for?" he asked Cash, barely containing his annoyance.

"Yes," Cash said simply, offering no explanation. I really needed to take lessons from this man on being the powerful one in a conversation, I thought.

"You know she's a…psychic, right? A kook? I would be careful with her," Theodore said and my mouth dropped open.

"Careful there, Theodore, or I'll tell the whole room what color your underwear is," I said, smiling sweetly at Theodore.

His face turned an even darker shade of red and he began to puff, looking like a fish out of water.

"I'll have to ask you to go now, Theodore, as I'm on a date with this beautiful psychic, and insulting her is not part of my plan tonight," Cash said, holding Theodore's eyes before turning to reach for my hand and bringing it to his lips.

A snort of laughter escaped me and I waited to see how Theodore would respond.

"Yes, so sorry to disturb you. I hope we can have that meeting this week," Theodore said weakly and turned, not bothering to acknowledge me as he bumped through the tables, barreling his way to the door.

Cash raised an eyebrow at me.

"What color underwear am *I* wearing?" he asked, and all the embarrassment that Theodore had caused slipped from me and was replaced with a very healthy zing of lust.

"I guess I'll have to find out," I said, looking up at him in what I hoped was a very sexy manner.

"I look forward to it," Cash said, with a husky timbre in his voice that made me shiver.

"Excuse me," the waitress said and I jumped back, pulling my hand from his as bowls of crabs were dropped in front of us.

"So, are you an only child?" Cash asked and I breathed out a little, glad the tension had passed, grateful that Cash hadn't made a big deal of Theodore being a jerk.

"Yes, I am. Okay, question…you were supposed to have dinner with Theodore tonight?" I asked, wanting clarification on Janelle's little rant earlier in the day.

"With him and his wife and another couple," Cash said, spearing a piece of crab with his fork. "They are interested in maybe buying into the condo development."

Huh. Looked like Janelle hadn't actually had a real date with Cash. Which made me wonder why she wanted to make it seem like she had…

"So an only child…" Cash prompted.

"Oh, yes, an only child to a professor of music and a world-renowned psychic. My childhood was colorful, eclectic, and exactly what I needed."

"Wait…Rose. Is your mom *the* Abigail Rose?" Cash said, his mouth dropping open.

"The one and only," I said, breaking off another piece of cornbread, watching Cash absorb the news.

"Wow, she's famous. So that would mean…your gift is just as strong as hers?"

"She's better in some respects. She's been doing it longer too," I said.

"I'm so fascinated by all of this. Kudos to you for continuing the family tradition and making money from it," Cash said, raising his glass to me in a toast.

"Well, thank you. Not everyone is always that excited about my gift," I admitted.

"Sure, I suspect it can be off-putting for some people," Cash said. "Either people who have something to hide or aren't comfortable with themselves."

"That's an excellent assessment, sir," I said, tilting my head at him and appraising him more deeply. It wasn't often that someone could size up the nuances that came with being a psychic.

"You'll have to give me a reading sometime," Cash said.

"I'd love to. So, gay brother? Tell me about your family," I said, wanting to learn more about him.

"Three brothers and one younger sister who constantly defies our wishes," Cash said, his eyes lighting up as he talked about his family. "My dad runs a construction company and I've worked with him off and on through the years. Mom's an attorney and as sharp as a tack. There is no crossing that woman."

"Sounds like you all love each other a lot," I said.

"We do. You'll meet them soon enough as I'm sure they'll follow me down here to check out what I'm getting into," Cash said and signaled to the waitress.

My mouth went dry at his casual assumption that I would meet his family. Was he already talking about a future together? Clamping down on the giddiness I felt rising up, I tried to get out of my head and live in the moment. One date did not equal a future together. I barely knew this man.

"Do you like horror movies?" I asked, interrupting him.

"Horror movies? God no," Cash said.

"Me either," I said, feeling a little sense of relief.

"How do you feel about *Mad Men*?" he asked, figuring out what I was doing.

"Ugh, so dry. Hate it," I admitted.

"Me too!"

We both laughed and clinked our glasses again. The sun had set and a rosy glow from the candles made our table seem more intimate. Cash leaned over the table until his face was closer to mine.

"I'd like to have another drink," he said.

"Okay," I said, staring into his light eyes.

"At your house," he said, his look full of meaning.

"Oh, um, yes, sure, I'd like that," I said, mentally kicking myself for stumbling over my words.

"I'll get the check."

A million thoughts battered my nervous brain on the car ride home. I kept thinking about if I had made my bed or if I had my cute bra on. Nerves skittered through my stomach and I did my best to keep up the conversation until Cash pulled his Jeep up in front of my house. Sitting in the front seat, waiting for Cash to open the door, I blew out a breath.

"Shall we?" Cash said, holding my door open for me.

"We shall," I said, smiling up at him and allowing him to pull me from the car. I brushed past him, not meeting his eyes, knowing he wanted to kiss me but not being willing to give our neighbors a show. Looking up, I saw a blind twitch and groaned to myself. The gossip mills would be churning.

Mental note – Cash's car couldn't be out front all night, I thought as I unlocked the door and immediately bent to pet Hank who was doing his crazy welcome home barks.

"He's a feisty guy, huh?"

"Yes and no. He's either all on or totally off," I said as I moved to the kitchen, turning on lights along the way. I gestured towards a couch.

"Have a seat, I'll bring you a beer?"

"Perfect," Cash said, easing onto a red couch and bending over to pet Hank. Hank immediately jumped up next to him and circled three times before curling into a ball next to Cash.

I sighed as I walked over and watched Cash stroke Hank's back. I knew that I should make Cash go, but he was just making it so hard not to want a taste of him.

"Here you go," I said, handing him a beer and setting my glass on the table in front of him as I eased onto the couch next to Cash, turning a bit and pulling one knee up beside me.

Cash leaned over and put his drink on the table before turning to me.

I swear the temperature went up by ten degrees as he

moved closer to me, placing one hand beside my arm and the other on my waist.

"I don't like small talk," Cash said, moving until his lips hovered inches from mine.

"Me either," I whispered and then in a flash, he slid his lips over mine, pulling me into his heat.

Raw power and edgy lust shot over me and I lowered my mental shields, allowing myself to revel in the essence of Cash, getting more turned on by being able to read just how much he wanted me. His seduction was level expert, and I was going down for the count.

Ffffppppt!

Oh shit.

Cash pulled away from me, both eyebrows raised as I bit my bottom lip and tried desperately not to laugh.

"Was that Hank?" Cash asked incredulously. His nose crinkled as Hank's gift wafted over him.

"We'd better move," I suggested, my shoulders shaking with laughter, as Cash and I made a beeline for the kitchen.

"I can't...that little thing? Wow," Cash said, laughing so hard he had to wipe tears from his eyes.

"Bostons are known for being gassy. I'm sorry, I should have warned you," I gasped, bending over at the waist as I howled with laughter.

Who needed a chaperone to cool you down when you had Hank?

Cash leaned companionably next to me at the counter, turning to look at me.

"So, where were we before we were so rudely interrupted?" he asked, his eyes hooded, his voice husky with lust.

"Hold up," I said, bracing my hand on his chest.

"Jeez," I said, distracted by the hard muscles under my palm. I started to trace my hand down his chest to his abs and then froze.

"Whoops, sorry."

"Go ahead and explore," Cash said, his smile wicked.

I backed up and crossed my hands behind my back.

"I shouldn't. We shouldn't. Lord do I want to go upstairs with some chocolate sauce for dessert, but we shouldn't. Not yet. I need time," I heard myself saying, even though my body screamed its protest.

"You say no, but that dessert idea sounded pretty damn good," Cash said.

"Sorry, I blurt things out when I'm nervous," I said, backing up another foot. I may be stupid sometimes, but I'd had enough warning signs this week that something bad was about to go down. For all I knew, Cash was a part of it.

Hell, it could even be about Cash and me.

Knowing it was best to not get too involved quite yet, I smiled up at Cash.

"Rain check?"

Cash moved in and slid his hands to my waist, pulling me until I was pressed against his hard length. I gasped but couldn't help running my hands up his arms to wrap around his shoulders.

"I'm going to hold you to that," he said against my lips before kissing me until I almost – almost – said screw it, meet me upstairs in five minutes.

I'd be lying if I said that I wasn't shaky after he stepped away and strolled casually to the front door, calling goodbye to Hank, taking all of his power and heat with him.

"What have I gotten myself into?" I said out loud and turned, downing my glass of wine in one gulp.

I foresaw another restless night in my future.

See? I told you I was a good psychic.

Chapter Ten

ON FRIDAY, LUNA came into my room as I was daydreaming about Cash and sat down in my client's chair with a huff. It had been two days since our date and Cash had called me the night before to talk, and we'd set a date for Saturday night dinner. Knowing that I'd been a bit preoccupied lately, I pushed thoughts of Cash aside and narrowed in on Luna.

Her stick-straight blonde hair was tucked in a messy ponytail, and her gray shift dress was wrinkled.

"What's wrong with you?" I gasped, watching as she tapped her fingers on the table. I couldn't believe that I'd missed her wrinkly dress when I had come into the shop this morning.

The only thing that came between Luna and her iron was a man.

"Renaldo?" I asked, realizing that she'd yet to fill me in on her date with him. What a bad friend I was being this week, I thought with shock. "Luna, I'm sorry, I can't believe I didn't ask you about your date."

Luna waved her hand distractedly. "It's fine. It's nice to see you mooning over a guy for once."

That stopped me.

"I am most certainly not mooning," I said stiffly.

"I would know, as I'm the one who has been watching you moon, haven't I?" Luna said, a note of tension in her voice.

Deciding to pick my battles, I backed down.

"Tell me about your date," I said, moving to sit across from her at the table.

"It was great. Everything was great. Or so I thought…"

"Where did you go?"

"We went up to Key Largo and had this amazing dinner on a private yacht that he said he knew the owners of. It was perfect, quite honestly. Sunset cruise, good music, great food, charming man…and, ah shit, I slept with him."

"You did!" I squealed. I couldn't help it. Usually it was the other way around – I was the one to rush headfirst into relationships while Luna proceeded exceedingly slowly, exercising caution with every twist and turn.

"I know. I don't know why, really. There was just something pushing me to have fun with him…you know, live a little," Luna said, a pleading note in her voice.

"Hey, no judgment here. If you had fun, that's all that matters," I said, holding my hands up to show her that I was on her side.

"Yeah, well it was a mistake, that jerk hasn't called me. I even broke down and texted him…but nada. Nothing. Zilch."

My senses went on full alert and I flashed back to Renaldo, fear in his eyes as he looked at the death card.

"Oh, this isn't good," I said.

"What? What do you mean?"

I looked at Luna helplessly. Should I break client confidentiality to tell her about his reading? She was my best friend after all.

"You think he got what he wanted and bailed, don't you?" Luna said, jumping up to pace my room.

She'd given me an easy out without realizing it. Deciding to wait just a little longer before I broke confidence, I nodded.

"Though it's hard to believe that any man would walk away from a woman like you, that just might be the case," I said, shrugging my shoulders. "Asshole," I added for emphasis.

"Ugh, I knew it!" Luna stabbed the air with her finger. "I knew it was a mistake to sleep with him."

"I'm sorry, girl. Want to watch a movie and eat chocolate tonight?" I said, immediately offering up the best friend fare for broken hearts.

"No, I'm fine. It isn't that bad. I mean, it is, but I can't say my heart is broken," Luna sighed and moved towards her side of the shop. "Which I guess is why I shouldn't have been sleeping with him, huh?"

I shrugged. "I think you just gotta take each man as he comes and figure it out," I said sagely.

Like I was an expert on relationships.

Chapter Eleven

I WAS UP before the birds – as the saying goes – on a Saturday morning, of all things. Not like I slept in much on Saturdays anyway, as I typically went into the shop for readings by 11:00.

Luna had taken me up on the offer of girl time and we'd had a fun night on the couch at her place, bitching about men and watching comedies. After a few hours, Luna's mood had lightened, and I could tell that she was back on track by the time I had left. Thankfully, it had stopped me from breaking confidentiality about Renaldo's reading.

Now if only Renaldo would make a damn appearance, I thought as I packed my dive bag. I had this niggling worry that something had happened to him and I just couldn't shake it.

"Stupid club guy probably went back to Miami to flash his money around," I told Hank, and he barked enthusiastically in agreement.

"Good boy," I said, smiling at his smushy face as I

fished another toy from his toy drawer. The toys weren't really new; I just rotated them so he would have some variety.

"Back in a bit," I called to Hank and breezed out the door, my dive bag slung over my shoulders and a loose cover-up pulled over my swimsuit. Hopping onto my bike, I pedaled through the quiet streets of Tequila, enjoying the morning silence. I wondered if Trace was going to give me a hard time about my date with Cash. I hadn't heard from him since our dive earlier this week, but that wasn't entirely unusual.

"Miss Althea!"

I jerked my head up and braked my bike, shading my eyes to look up at Miss Elva sweeping her front sidewalk in a flowing caftan the color of the sun at dusk.

I pulled my bike to the side of the road.

"Miss Elva. Always lovely to see you."

She turned, and looked me up and down.

"You don't have my gris-gris on you."

It was a statement, not a question and I felt my shoulders hunch a bit.

"Sorry, Miss Elva," I said, not able to meet her eyes.

"You need to carry that with you," she insisted.

"I can't take it with me at all times, like when I'm diving, but I promise to tuck it in my dive bag next time. I have it in my purse," I explained, wanting her to know that I valued her offering.

"Hmpf. The day you don't wear it is the day you will need it," Miss Elva promised and went back to her sweeping, muttering about my stupidity.

I bit my lip and turned to look back down the road.

Should I go back and get it? Checking my watch, I knew I would be cutting it close if I ran back to get the gris-gris before diving.

I rolled my eyes and continued on to the wharf. With all the voodoo, and the hoodoo, and the white witches going on around me, sometimes it was easy to get swept up in things. I'd spent my whole life without any gris-gris; I'm sure I would be just fine, I reasoned, allowing my practical side to shove its way to the top of my head.

The dock was humming with activity when I got there, as Saturdays were typically busy days for fishing charters. Locking my beach cruiser – painted hot pink of course – to the bike rack, I strolled down to Trace's boat, nodding good morning at people as I tried to push down the worry Miss Elva had managed to kick up.

A woman in a neon orange bikini caught my eye as I neared Trace's boat, and I slowed, wondering if he had a group booked for the day after all. Trace stood in front of her, his hair pulled back from his face with his sunglasses shading his eyes. A flirty laugh reached me and I groaned as the girl reached out and pushed Trace's chest a bit, laughing up at him. Trace didn't seem to mind. I mentally gagged.

"Hey!" I called, interrupting them as I reached the boat. The girl jumped a little, then turned to look at me with her lips pursed.

Oh, it's like that, I thought, as she looked me up and down and then raised an eyebrow before turning back to Trace.

"See you tonight?" she asked, not acknowledging my presence.

"Unless he has a date with me," I said, smiling as I stepped past them onto the boat, removing my shoes and moving across to the bench to pull my bag off my shoulders. I didn't look back, barely able to keep the snarky smile from my face. Hopefully that would be enough to put Orange Bikini in her place.

"Really, Thea?" Trace asked as he stepped onto the boat, annoyance lacing his voice.

"What? That girl is a bitch," I said, turning to defend myself.

"Sienna's just shy," he said, standing in front of me, his arms crossed.

"Sienna, is it? Well, I don't like all 90 pounds of her," I said with a huff as I turned and began to unpack my bag.

"Well that's too bad, I do," Trace shot back as he moved behind the wheel. "Can you get the ropes?"

"Fine," I said, pulling my cover-up off and sauntering across the front of the boat to jump on the dock. I made sure to bend over to give Trace the best view of my skimpy bikini. He could like 90-pound skinny girls all he wanted, but I wasn't going to hide what a real woman looked like either, I thought with satisfaction as I heard him curse.

The boat's engines roared and I jumped on the front as Trace reversed, and made my way back to the shaded part of the boat where the dive gear was.

"Cute," Trace called over the engines and I bit my lip, hiding a grin.

"I thought you liked this bikini," I called, and then shook my head at myself. Why was I courting trouble when I had a man like Cash taking me out for dinner tonight? The thought of Cash, and the heat his mouth gave me, sobered me instantly.

"I like what the bikini is on," Trace called back and then set his GPS. Turning, he looked at me. "What? Date didn't go well with Investor Boy? Looking to slum it with the likes of me?"

My mouth dropped open as a protest rose to my lips.

"Dating you is not slumming, Trace. Why would you think that?"

"Dude clearly has more money than me. Not to mention he looks like a freaking movie star," Trace grumbled.

"Trace, you're a great guy. Plenty of women would be lucky to have you."

"So why not you?" Trace said, his gaze on me.

The question left me frozen as I had to honestly consider it. My mouth worked to form an answer, but I couldn't really come up with one. There was no reason that I wouldn't date Trace. So why wouldn't I?

Trace waved his hand at me.

"Never mind, don't answer that. We've always had piss-poor timing." He shrugged and took a swig from his water bottle.

We did?

That was news to me. Had I been involved in a game of romantic missed-chances with Trace and never even known it? I needed to talk to Luna; she was good at dissecting this stuff.

"So the date?" Trace asked, biting out the words.

"Great. It was great. He's a good guy," is all I said, not

sure if my words were hurting him, torn on what I was supposed to do in a situation like this.

"Good. If he treats you bad, tell him I'll kick his ass," Trace said dryly.

I stood and walked over to Trace, leaning in to his tall frame to wrap an arm around his waist.

"You're a good one, Trace," I said softly, looking up at him.

"Careful, Althea. Putting your arm around me in that skimpy bikini is only going to lead to the type of trouble that I'm just not sure you can handle," Trace said, his words causing me to gasp and step back, while a low tug of lust rocketed through my body.

"And it's clear that you're not as indifferent to me as I thought," Trace said, raising an eyebrow as he looked down at my breasts, where the thin bathing suit material offered a clear indication that I was turned on.

I took a deep breath and stepped back, moving away from Trace and the threat – or was it a promise – that he offered. Busying myself with my dive gear, I tried to think of Cash and how nice it would be to see him again tonight.

Not about the fact that I was alone on a boat with a very sexy man who had just declared his very serious interest in seeing what was beneath my bathing suit.

"Do you want to dive the wall again? We can go further south, where there are those crazy tunnels and it drops off forever," Trace called and I blew out a breath, tamping down the lust that still surged inside of me.

"Yes, I'd love that."

"Cool, we'll be there in five then," Trace said, turning the boat a bit. I sat on the bench and looked out of the back of the boat, watching our trail through the water away from the mainland. The water was the bright turquoise so particular to the Caribbean, and the land was just a thin strip of golden sand and green trees in the distance. It made my heart hurt, just a little, to look at it. Sure, we had to deal with hurricanes and tropical storms, but on days like this, I wouldn't want to live anywhere else in the world.

I stood up and stepped into my wetsuit, shimmying it over my bathing suit and shoving my arms into the sleeves before stepping to the front of the boat as the large orange buoy bobbed in the water in front of us. I grabbed the hook pole and leaned over to snag the buoy line and secure the boat.

"All good?"

"Yes, let's dive," I said, moving to the back of the boat.

"Okay, so at this site, we'll drop to the top of the wall and go to the left through a sand chute that will lead into a tunnel. The tunnel comes out over the drop-off. We'll drop down to about 120 feet along the wall; there are some super cool ledges that jut out randomly along the way that we can look under."

"Sounds good. I remember this dive; should be good for some pictures," I said, snagging my camera to put by my feet as I slid my BCD on and tightened the straps of the vest. Bending forward, I stepped from the bench, the weight of the tank heavy at my back as I made my way to the seat at the back of the boat where I secured my fins and my mask before standing up, camera in one hand.

"All good?" Trace asked again as I paused before entering the water.

"Yes, I think so," I said, suddenly feeling very unnerved. I ran my hand over my BCD again, checking straps, weights, and looking at my computer to see how much air I had in the tank.

"You sure?" Trace asked, watching me.

"Yeah, Miss Elva gave me the heebie-jeebies on the way over here, is all," I said, waving it away.

Trace burst out in laughter, his eyes lighting behind his mask.

"She runs a good game, but I'm not entirely convinced she knows what's what," he said.

"I'm not so sure about that, but I'll take your word for it today. I'm ready," I said, putting the regulator to my mouth. Trace gave me the go ahead and I waited for the boat to dip low before doing a giant stride into the water, holding my mask and reg to my face with one hand and clutching my camera in the other.

The cool blue water welcomed me home and I sighed in happiness as Trace and I shot an "OK" signal to each other and began our descent to the sand chute below us. I couldn't help but watch how gracefully Trace moved through the water, his lean muscles outlined in his wetsuit.

Jeez, I was ready to just give it away all over town, I thought and shook my head, focusing back on the ocean bottom as we arrived near the sand and adjusted our buoyancy so we could swim neutrally through the water. Trace motioned me towards a tunnel that cut through the coral and my heart picked up speed a little bit. There was such a rush exploring tunnels at seventy feet, not knowing what you would find at the other end. I pulled my regulator hoses in close to me so as not to catch the coral and began to ease my way through the tunnel, taking pictures of a lobster that poked its spiny head out at us.

We reached the end of the tunnel and floated out over the blue abyss, my favorite part. I would challenge anyone not to feel a rush of excitement hovering above a 4,000-foot drop-off that faded into nothing. There could be anything down there...

I pulled out of my thoughts as Trace motioned for me to follow him over the coral wall and down to about 120 feet. I checked my dive computer and, knowing I only had about eight minutes at this depth, I brought my camera up and began to shoot pictures as we moved along the wall, coming upon a series of ledges sticking out from the wall like spikes. My eye caught a turtle moving up the coral between two ledges so I kicked ahead of Trace, determined to get a good picture. Holding the camera in front of me as I rounded a ledge, I fired off shot after shot, racing to catch the turtle.

And came up short on a scream as Renaldo's bloated head swooped into my field of vision, the flash from my camera highlighting the deathly pallor of his skin.

A jerk on my fin had me screaming into my regulator again, as panic raced up my spine and clawed at my throat, tearing the air from my mouth.

Chapter Twelve

I WHIRLED, READY to do battle, only to find Trace pulling me to him, turning me from Renaldo and pinching my hand, forcing me to look into his eyes. Tears blurred my vision as I struggled to catch my breath to fight down the panic attack that so desperately wanted to take over my body. Trace reached out and held his hand over my regulator, making sure I kept it lodged in my mouth.

Losing my shit at 120 feet would be a quick way to die.

I blinked the tears back and forced my breathing to become shallow and slow. Trace watched me, keeping an eye on my bubbles to see how quickly I was expelling air. He reached over to pull my computer to him to see how much air was left in the tank before he motioned to my hand.

Confused, I held up my camera in question.

Nodding, Trace took the camera from me and then flashed me the okay sign.

I realized that he wanted to take pictures of the body.

It felt like my heart was clambering to get out of my chest, but I nodded. Trace was a search-and-rescue diver, so this was not his first rodeo. I moved behind him, reaching out to hold a piece of rock on the wall to steady myself as I took a closer look at the scene.

Murder scene, I should add as the details of Renaldo's final gruesome moments became apparent. The term "sleeping with the fishes" had just taken on a very real meaning for me.

I flinched as the flash seemed to make Renaldo's body jerk, and I shivered inside my suit, trying desperately to swallow the bile that threatened to rise in my throat.

Renaldo bobbed gently in the water, a chain affixed to his ankle, a heavy anchor locked to the end of the chain. Red marks radiated up his leg where he must have tried to claw his way out of the chain as the anchor sank over the drop-off. His clothing billowed loosely around him and I cringed as I saw a fish swim up and take a nibble at his mouth.

The sea never rejected free food, I thought dimly, knowing that I was about two beats away from giggling hysterically into my mask.

Trace turned and nodded at me, signaling to go up the wall.

I took one last glance at Renaldo and said the only Catholic prayer that I knew as my eyes found the gold cross at his throat. He hadn't deserved this, I thought as I turned and began to follow Trace up the wall.

Or had he?

There was very little I knew about him aside from that my best friend jumped his bones the other night. My reading for him had revealed nothing aside from a deep-rooted fear.

And that is precisely what I need to figure out, I thought as we reached our fifteen-foot safety stop where we would stay for the next several minutes, allowing decompression to work on our bodies. I swam in mindless circles as I thought about his fear from the other day.

Renaldo had known that he needed to leave his job. It had been clear from his question, and the fear surrounding it, that something had happened with his work to make him scared. Wishing he had listened to my suggestion that he leave his work, guilt began to creep up on me as I wondered if I had done enough to prevent his death. Tremors began to rack my body as the full effect of what I had just seen washed over me. I needed to get out of the water. Now.

Cutting my safety stop a few seconds short, I swam for the ladder and took my fins off, chucking them onto the boat and pulling myself up. I waddled over to the bench and sat, desperate to have my tank off, needing to just let it all out as I slipped from the bench to the floor.

Wrapping my arms around my knees, I buried my head in my thighs as the shaking overtook me and I bawled into the little ball of safety I had made. I heard Trace get on the boat but didn't look up, couldn't speak – couldn't think – as I continued to tremble, sobs seeming to tear from deep inside me.

"Thea," Trace said, coming to sit on the ground next to me. He wrapped his arms around the ball I had made and pulled me into his lap. A dim part of my mind was surprised at his strength, but instead I let him hug me, needing his warmth.

Needing to feel alive.

"That's so messed up," I blurted out, my teeth chattering.

"I know. Trust me, I know. It's awful. I've…well, I've seen a lot of dead bodies. But never a murder," Trace said.

I craned my head to look at him, meeting his beautiful blue eyes that were filled with sadness.

"How do you do it? How do you see that and remain unaffected?"

"I'm always affected. It makes me incredibly sad. I just try to look at it as a service to the family and to the deceased. I believe they would want me to find them…to give closure to their story."

"I don't think I could do it," I whispered.

"It's part of what makes me so desperate to live my life to the fullest. Sure, I could be making a ton of money being in a cubicle somewhere in New York or going into investing, but I chose to live my life doing the things that I love. I consider it a tribute to the bodies I've found that don't get that chance anymore," Trace said, his mouth at my ear as I stared out at the water, the boat bobbing in the waves.

"I could have saved him," I blurted out and then stilled, waiting to hear what Trace would say, wanting to know if he would judge me.

"You know him?" Trace's voice went up several octaves.

"Yes, his name's Renaldo. He was working with an

investment group or something. Luna just had a date with him."

"Oh shit," Trace said, his voice heavy with emotion.

"I gave him a reading. He wanted one…and he was just full of fear. Like it radiated from him. He asked if he should leave his job and go home. And then he pulled the death card. And it was the first time in all of my readings that I knew the death card really meant he was going to die. I urged him to leave his job, but I didn't tell him that he would die. I just – I couldn't, you know?" I said, turning to look at Trace again, pleading my case.

He ran his hand down my arm and pulled me tighter to his chest, pressing my face into his neck.

"Shh, this isn't your fault. Whatever the hell he got mixed up in is what caused this. You told him to leave. He didn't take your warning. There's nothing else you could have done. You didn't cause this," Trace reassured me.

I hung on to those words as we waited on the boat for the Coast Guard to arrive. Trace handed me a banana and insisted that I eat it as he continued to make calls to the local police and the Coast Guard. I could see their boats in the distance, three of them, coming at us like a wave of doom.

You didn't cause this.

Trace's words floated through my mind and I reminded myself, again, that this wasn't my fault.

"She was right," I said bitterly as I took a swig of water from my bottle, my eyes trained on the boats on the horizon.

"Who was?" Trace pulled the phone away from his head and looked at me.

"Miss Elva. She was right. The day you don't have your gris-gris bag is the day you need it."

Trace just shook his head at me and went back to his call as I closed my eyes against the promise of awfulness that the three boats on the horizon carried.

It was going to be a long day.

Chapter Thirteen

THE BOBBING OF the boat was beginning to make me a little sick, though I couldn't be certain it wasn't from the fact that I had just seen my first dead body.

Well, not technically my first, I thought as I flashed back to my great-grandmother's funeral when I was ten years old. I remembered the weight of sadness from the people in the room, and my shock at seeing my lifeless nana laid out in a coffin. At the time, all I had wanted to do was pull her from the coffin and force-feed her baked goods until she returned to being the sweet nana I had known.

Shaking the memory from my head, I focused on Trace, who was speaking with the Coast Guard and the local police at the back of the boat. The trio of men kept casting glances my way.

"What?" I finally asked, rising from where I huddled on the bench with a towel over my shoulders to go stand with them.

"Thea, you know Chief Dupree," Trace said, gesturing

to the town's chief of police. A large mustache snaked across his face, just beginning to curl at the tips, and mirrored aviators concealed his eyes.

"Chief," I said, nodding at him and trying to decide if I wanted to take a dip into his thoughts or not.

"And this is Senior Chief Petty Officer Thomas," Trace said, declaring the rank of the man who stood next to him.

I smiled at him and held out my hand. "Althea Rose."

A white smile flashed briefly in a tanned face, his blond hair cut military short and Oakleys shading his eyes. He was built like a tank and stood like he was ready to salute at any moment.

"Ma'am," Chief Thomas said, politely addressing me, and I liked him immediately. He seemed to give off an "I can take care of this" confidence that I admired.

"So, what's the consensus? Do you need to take a statement?" I asked, not sure what the procedure in a situation like this was. I pulled the towel more tightly around me, trying to comfort myself like I was diving under my blankets at home.

"Yes, we'll need to take a statement and look at those photos that Trace said he took," Chief Dupree drawled.

"If Trace has his laptop out here, I can hook the camera to it and pull the pictures," I offered and Chief Thomas smiled.

"We'd be mighty appreciative of that. We just have one other problem at the moment," Chief Thomas said.

"What's that?"

"We need to bring the body up," Trace said, turning to meet my eyes and I suddenly realized why they had been side-eyeing me before.

"You want me to go back down?" I squeaked.

"I can do it alone," Trace protested and Chief Thomas just shook his head at him.

"You know you can't go down alone."

"You're absolutely right you can't! Not at that depth," I protested. I moved closer to Trace and he automatically reached out and put an arm around my shoulders, rubbing his hand on my back to soothe me.

"Aren't you the Coast Guard? And the police? Don't you have someone who can do this?" I asked defensively and Chief Dupree sighed and shook his head.

"Trace is a search-and-rescue diver, if I need to remind you, Althea," Chief Dupree said, tugging on his mustache. "The boat's here, we have the dry lift bags, the scene has been photographed. We just need the body."

I shivered, thinking about going back down to see Renaldo's body eerily floating in the water, the fish enjoying him as a meal.

"Aren't you a diver?" I asked Chief Thomas, a little angry that he seemed to be belying my impression of him as a Take Charge Man.

"I am, but unfortunately I just came from two recovery dives this morning. I'm at surface for at least two hours," he explained.

"So can't we wait?" I asked, not wanting to go through this with Trace, not wanting him to have to go through it either.

"Thea, let's just do this. You've already seen the worst of it. You'll be better prepared for it when we go down," Trace said.

"I don't know if I'll ever be prepared for seeing a

murdered body," I spat out and moved away to where my wetsuit was laid out in the sun.

"Why do you say he was murdered?" Chief Dupree asked.

"Gee, I don't know? Maybe the chain around his ankle along with the anchor attached?" I shot over my back as I shrugged the towel off and quickly slipped into my wetsuit, trying to minimize the time that I stood in my bikini around the men.

"One can't make assumptions," Chief Dupree said and I whirled on him.

"Oh? You think this is a suicide? What a joke," I said, my eyes wide in disbelief.

Chief Dupree shrugged.

"We won't declare anything until we have cause of death," he explained.

"You've got to be kidding me," I muttered, turning back to check my dive computer to see if I was clear to dive again, hating Chief Dupree in that moment.

"I've got my laptop here," Trace said and I nodded, reaching into the freshwater bin to pull my camera out and detach it from the rig. Using my towel to wipe the camera off, I silently handed it to Trace, confident that he knew how to transfer the photos.

Watching as the men huddled around the computer, I sat on the bench and dropped my shields, not caring if I was intruding on their mental privacy. I had a murder to solve, didn't I?

I slipped into Chief Thomas' mind and caught a glimpse of him carefully considering every aspect of the pictures he was seeing, while running procedures in his head before I lost the image. Moving on, I tried to get a read on Chief Dupree's thoughts and my eyebrows rose as a flash of his thoughts reached me.

Make this go away.

What the hell?

I couldn't understand why Chief Dupree would want to squash this. Tequila Key hadn't had a murder case in years. I would think he'd be juiced up to do something other than fining tourists for littering and giving out the occasional speeding ticket. What was he hiding, I wondered, glaring at him as he tugged on his mustache again.

"From my estimation, I would say this looks like murder," Chief Thomas finally said and I nodded at him, putting him back into the man-who-gets-things-done category.

"Oh? Are you a coroner?" Chief Dupree asked, and the other man turned to look at him.

"No, but I've seen my fair share of murdered bodies over the years, and this reeks of foul play," Chief Thomas said.

"See!" I couldn't help but exclaim and the men all turned to me.

"What?" I asked, raising my shoulders.

Trace sighed and moved back from the computer, walking over to crouch in front of me. I searched his eyes, wishing we didn't have to deal with this.

"You okay to do this?"

"I have to be," I said, my voice flat.

"Then let's talk about what has to be done," Chief Thomas said and I turned to look at him.

"Sorry you have to do this, Ms. Rose," he added and I

offered him a half smile, nodding my acknowledgement. "You'll need to take bolt cutters down to snap the chain. After that, you'll need a lift bag for the body and a lift bag for the anchor. We'll want to preserve as much evidence as we can."

I grimaced as I thought about the work we would have to do to get Renaldo's body to the surface, but nodded my understanding. Silently, I slipped my arms into my BCD vest, strapping it closed and slinging my mask onto my head. Trace had already rigged up new tanks for us, but I double-checked my dive computer to be sure that I had air. Trace did the same and together we stood, hobbling to the back of the boat awkwardly with the tanks on our back, until we could sit and put on our fins.

"Do you need any more pictures?" I asked over my shoulder.

"No," Chief Dupree said.

I was handed two lift bags from Chief Thomas and Trace got another lift bag and a bolt cutter. We looked at each other and when the boat dipped low into the water, we jumped.

I bobbed for a moment at the surface, flashing an OK sign to Chief Thomas on the boat. Watching them for a second, panic flashed through me.

What if Miss Elva hadn't been warning me about finding a body? What if these two men were in on it and they were about to drive off in our boat? Leaving us stranded in the ocean? I gasped as these questions whirled in my mind, my breath coming in little puffs as I tried to debate whether we should continue our descent.

"Hey, what's wrong?" Trace asked, having swum to my side. Turning to look at him, I just shook my head.

"I think I'm going a little crazy. I was just imagining what would happen if they drove off in our boat and left us here."

Trace laughed and then sobered instantly.

"Is that what you read on them?" he asked, his blue eyes serious behind his mask.

I thought back to my previous impressions.

"I don't trust Dupree. Thomas seems like a solid dude. Plus he looks like he would take Dupree down in two seconds if he tried anything."

"Okay. If you're sure?"

Coming to a resolution, I nodded and then flashed the men on the boat another OK. Turning to put my face in the water, I clamped my mouth over the regulator and began my descent.

This time as I floated into the underwater world, I thought about how unforgiving the sea was. What was typically my oasis had shown her sinister side today. It was something that I was constantly reminded of – one must have a healthy respect for the ocean, as she threatens as much as she soothes.

A fickle woman is the sea.

We reached the bottom and I mechanically followed Trace along the sand chute and through the tunnel, barely paying attention to the same lobster that jutted out from his ledge to see what all the bubbles were about. Swimming out over the drop-off, I stared down into the deep blue abyss that yawned beneath me, knowing that but for a few feet of rocky outcropping, Renaldo's body would've been lost forever. I wondered how many others had succumbed to the same fate, coming to rest thousands of feet below us in a world yet undiscovered.

Snapping out of it, I looked up to see Trace waiting patiently for me. He motioned for me to follow him over the ledge and down along the wall to where the rocky ledges spiked out from the wall. As we neared where Renaldo's body was, I felt my shoulders begin to tense again.

You've already seen this. It can't get worse than what it already is, I reminded myself.

We turned the corner just as a grouper pulled Renaldo's eyeball from his face. I shrieked into my regulator before turning away, forcing myself to breathe normally.

Mary had a little lamb, Mary had a little lamb, I sang to myself in my head, forcing my thoughts away from what I had just seen.

This is what happens in the ocean, I reminded myself. *You know this. Now put your big girl panties on and turn around so Trace doesn't have to do this himself.*

Turning, I flashed the OK sign to Trace and then moved to where he had positioned himself by the chain connected to the anchor. Pulling out his lift bag, he attached one end to the anchor. Then he motioned to me and I pulled my lift bags from where I had tucked them in my BCD and turned to look at Renaldo. Gulping a little, I reached out to gingerly touch his pant leg, moving my hand up until I found his belt. I swallowed tightly, unable to look up at his face as I secured the two lift bags to his body. Two lift bags was probably overkill, but I didn't care if we lost the anchor. There was no way I was racing after

Renaldo's body if it dropped from the bag and sank into the abyss.

I moved back as Trace swam to my two lift bags and pulled a pony tank from his side. Pony tanks are small emergency tanks with a mouthpiece attached to the tank. They are useful to have in emergencies, as the tank is easy to transport or be brought down to someone who ran out of air. In this instance, Trace was slowly filling the lift bags attached to Renaldo's belt. I shuddered as the body jerked, bowing backward from the waist as the lift bags pulled it towards the surface.

Trace moved back, floating towards the feet where he repeated the process of filling the bag at the anchor. Once he clipped the chain, we'd each be responsible for getting our burden to the surface. I'd been assigned the anchor as it weighed slightly less than the body, and also because there was a high probability of me vomiting if I had to hold onto Renaldo's sea-ravaged body for more than a few seconds.

Grabbing one side of the chain, Trace wrapped it around his arm and then positioned the bolt cutters to do their job. I grimaced as I heard the snap and then moved to grab the anchor, waiting as Trace snagged Renaldo by his belt and together, we swam towards the surface.

And brought Renaldo's body to the light.

Chapter Fourteen

THE NEXT HOUR fell into a rhythm of routine and procedures. The banality of death struck me as I watched the police work – taking pictures, making marks, and writing in little notepads. Crime shows seemed to glamorize the procedure, but now I realized how painstakingly slow and unexciting it could be. No detail could be missed, everything must be cataloged. One slip on their part and a killer could be out the door and on his way to Mexico.

Trace moved to sit next to me, his shoulder bumping mine. I leaned into him, appreciating just how solid he had been today.

"Thanks," I said.

"For what?"

"For being you. For not letting me fall apart down there," I said, waving at the water. I turned to meet his eyes. "I was close, you know."

"I know. I could see it in your eyes. You rallied though," Trace said, his gaze holding mine. The moment lengthened between us, time suspended as I stared into the blue of his eyes, lost in the abyss much as I had been hours before.

"Hey, lovebirds," Chief Dupree called out and I jumped, heat rushing to my cheeks as I turned to glare at the police officer.

"You're all cleared to go. I've got your statements. Don't plan any sudden trips, hear me?" Dupree tugged on his mustache and I rose, my hands at my hips.

"And why is that? You think we murdered this poor man and then helped you bring him up? That's ridiculous!" Fury made my voice shake and tears threatened at the edges of my eyes.

"I didn't say that," Chief Dupree began.

"You listen up, Dupree. I'm going to find this killer and serve him up to you on a platter," I spat out, turning as Trace pulled my arm.

"What? He's an idiot," I seethed.

"Just let it go," Trace said, running his hands down my arms, forcing me to look up at his eyes. "He's got to follow up on every avenue."

"Please, he wants to hang this on someone and I'm telling you right now, it's not going to be me."

Turning, I looked at Chief Dupree again.

"You'd better be on the ball with this one, Dupree. It's not going to go away however much you would like it to."

Chief Dupree's shoulders went back and I swear his nostrils flared as though he was sniffing out a predator.

"I'll be the one giving orders, Ms. Rose, and the order is that you stay in town until this is all settled," he bit out before turning to jump back onto his boat.

"Jerk," I seethed to Trace as he started the engine on his boat.

"Just get the buoy, Thea. It's been a long day and you need to get your shit together because you still haven't told Luna about this."

Luna.

My heart froze as I thought about how I would tell Luna that her most recent lover was now in a body bag, tucked under a bench on a police boat currently speeding towards the docks.

I couldn't call her, I thought as I unhooked the boat from the buoy and walked back to pack my dive bag. I'd have to go find her, tell her in person. It was the only thing I could do.

We sat in silence as the boat approached the wharf. There wasn't much to say after a day like today. The police boat had already reached the main dock and I could see a crowd beginning to form. In a small town like Tequila Key, a police boat at the dock was like throwing a match on kerosene. The word would be across town in seconds.

Trace moved his boat onto a dock further down from where the crowd with the police boat was. There was no point in becoming involved with that little circus, as people would sniff out our involvement in finding the body soon enough.

"Run!" Trace joked, bringing some levity to the situation and I smiled at him as I pulled the straps of my bag over my shoulders.

"Trace, I really do need to run. I have to tell Luna about this before word gets to her."

"Go, go, I've got this."

I stopped in front of him and leaned up, wrapping my arms around him and kissing him softly on the cheek.

"I love you, you know," I whispered in his ear.

Trace pulled back and looked at me, his lips hovering inches from mine.

"You too. We'll continue this later," he said, before turning at the last instant and kissing my cheek. My stomach tumbled over at the brush of his lips and I wondered what this would mean for our friendship or if we had crossed into something more.

My life was so messed up right now, I thought as I stepped off the boat, lifting my eyes from my feet.

And looked into familiar gray eyes.

I froze as I looked at Cash, huddled on the back of a fancy fishing boat with Theodore Whittier, who was taking a delivery bag out of Luca's hands, along with two other men that I didn't recognize. The group reeked of money and prestige and something about it made my lip curl. I wondered what Cash had seen of my embrace with Trace and if he was jealous at all. I waved my hand at him, and he nodded at me, not moving. Theodore turned to see who Cash was looking at and then glared when he saw it was me, leaning in to whisper something in Cash's ear.

A wave of evil slapped me in the face, so powerful that I almost doubled over. I whipped my head around, trying to use my sixth sense to see where it was coming from. Ignoring Cash, I closed my eyes for a moment to concentrate, turning my head towards where I was certain the man responsible for Renaldo's death stood.

And opened my eyes to see that I was staring at Cash

and Theodore, both of whom were cocking their heads at me like I was crazy.

Unable to breathe, I put my head down and moved one foot in the front of the other as the truth settled, much like the anchor chained to Renaldo's leg, onto my shoulders.

The killer was somebody I knew.

Chapter Fifteen

I HOPPED ON my bike and tore away from the wharf,
wanting to leave the sadness and intensity behind me as I
struggled to understand what I had just learned on the
dock. Keeping my eyes on the ground in front of me, I
rushed my bike down the street toward our shop, hoping
that Luna was still at work.

"Shit," I said, and whipped a quick u-turn and raced
my bike down another block, sweat beginning to trickle
down my back beneath the dive bag on my shoulders. I
skidded to a stop in front of a ramshackle house with a
wide wrap-around porch.

"Miss Elva!" I yelled, not caring who heard me. "Miss
Elva!"

"Shoosh, girl, you gonna get the whole neighborhood
running out here," Miss Elva called from around the side
of her house. I got off of my bike and walked over to
where she stood behind her chain-link fence, a vine of
flowers intertwined amidst the links. A thin sheen of sweat
covered Miss Elva's face and she wiped her forehead with

the back of her hand, the moisture dampening the gardening gloves she wore.

"You were right," I said stoically, coming to stand against the fence, intertwining my fingers among the links.

"Sure, I could have told you that, child," Miss Elva scoffed and then took a closer look at my face. "There's death on your face, honeychild. There's death right there that I see. Who was it?"

I told her everything, as I pressed into the fence, tears streaming down my face again as the aftershock of what I had been through hit me.

"It's gonna get worse before it gets better, child," Miss Elva said, reaching out to smooth my hair back from my face.

"I know it is," I whispered, "it's one of us."

"You come back to me after you tell Miss Luna what's what. We'll figure this out together," Miss Elva promised.

"Thanks, Miss Elva," I said, and pushed away from the fence, feeling marginally better.

"You wear that gris-gris now, girl," she called after me and I turned, smiling at her.

"Don't think I won't. I learned the hard way today," I said.

"Hmpf, that's right you did," Miss Elva said, shooing me on my way, already focusing back on her garden.

Moments later, I skidded to a stop in front of our shop, only to see that the lights were off. Unsure if Luna was hunkered down inside, I tried the door to find it locked. Sliding my key in, I opened the door and poked my head in.

"Luna? Are you here? It's an emergency!" I called,

knowing that she would never ignore those words. Silence greeted me and I eased back out, locking the door after me.

Next stop, Luna's condo, I thought as I eased myself onto the bike and began to pedal towards Luna's side of town, wishing I had eaten more today as my energy was beginning to lag.

Tired, I pulled up to her sleek unit and, not even getting off of my bike, opened my mind to scan her building, looking for her brain signature to see if she was inside.

"Shit," I swore, knowing that she wasn't inside. With little else to do, I turned my bike towards home, wanting to be on my couch with a stiff drink before I picked up the phone to tell Luna that her lover was dead.

A sticky wall of heat pressed against me as I rode through town, keeping my eyes trained ahead of me as people began to call out my name as I passed. Match to kerosene, I thought again as I ignored another person shouting at me, knowing that they had heard by now that I was one of the people who had brought Renaldo's body up.

Finally – *finally* – I reached my house, delighted to see that the press hadn't come knocking at my door just yet. Tilting my head, I looked at my house. Something was different.

No Hank's ears.

I jumped off my bike and ran to the door, finding it open.

"Hank!" I shouted, rushing inside only to come up short, my hand at my heart as Hank raced joyously to me from where the back door stood open to the outside.

"I'm back here. With tequila," Luna called and my shoulders slumped. I should have known that Luna would have heard the gossip by now and come to my house. We had exchanged keys to each other's homes years ago when we'd failed to secure a long-term significant other in our lives.

I wondered briefly if Luna was my significant other before I grabbed a glass from my cabinet and walked outside, unsure of what I would find.

"Hey, buddy," I said, bending over to tug a stick from Hank's mouth and toss it into the yard before turning to assess the damage.

Luna reclined on my outdoor couch, her linen dress a cacophony of wrinkles, her hair tied back in a messy bun. Mascara streaks under her eyes indicated recent tears, though her eyes were dry when they found mine.

"It was Renaldo, wasn't it?" she asked, her voice shaky.

I wanted to deny it, to save her from this pain, but I couldn't.

"Yes," I said simply, moving to drop wearily onto the couch next to her.

"I knew it. As soon as I heard that a body was found, I knew it was him. That's weird, isn't it?" Luna said dully and I just shrugged, leaning over to pour a shot of Don Julio from the chunky bottle that sat on the table. Squeezing a lime into it, I added a few ice cubes and brought the glass to my mouth, savoring the taste of the tequila, so sharp and sweet against my tongue.

"Not really. We do have some help in the extrasensory department," I said as I sat back, turning to put my arm around her. "I'm sorry, hon."

Luna returned my hug, holding me for a moment as a shudder wracked her thin frame.

"I wish I could make this better," I said against her hair.

Luna took a deep sigh and sat back, pushing a lock of her hair from her face.

"It's okay. I mean, it's totally awful and absolutely not okay, but it's not like he was my husband or something." Luna shrugged one dainty shoulder and leaned over to pour more tequila into her glass. I reached down to throw the stick again for Hank, allowing the day's events to catch up with me.

"Trace and I found him."

Luna gasped and turned, immediately pulling me to her chest, so that my drink sloshed over my glass.

"I didn't know. I hadn't heard that much. I just heard that the Coast Guard was bringing a dead body in. I swear I didn't know," she gushed, patting my back vigorously as I struggled to hold my drink.

"Luna, I'm spilling," I said gently and she eased back.

"Sorry. Oh my God, were you diving?" Luna said, her eyes wide, concern etched across her face.

"We were. I almost lost it at 120 feet," I said, launching into the story, grateful that this time my voice held as I recounted it.

"Murdered," Luna breathed, hanging on my words.

"Why, what do people think it was?" I asked, curious what the rumor mill was saying.

"Drowned," Luna said, leaning back to put her head on the cushion and stare up at the ceiling where my plantation fan made lazy swoops.

"Luna, this is bad. It's one of us. Someone here," I said, nervously tracing my hand up and down my glass, drawing lines through the perspiration on the side.

"Who is it?" Luna gasped, leaning forward to stare at me.

"I don't know. I just got a sense that the killer was on the dock. I…I…" I couldn't bring myself to say that it might be Cash.

A knock at the door stopped me.

"Shit, that's going to be reporters," I said, bringing my palms up to wipe at my eyes, knowing that I was going to look like crap on the front page of our weekly newspaper.

"I will handle this," Luna said firmly, standing up and marching – well, wobbling just a bit on her wedge espadrilles – to the front door.

Murmured voices reached me, but I was too tired to try and listen. Instead, I leaned back, resting my head on the cushion and smiling when Hank jumped up to curl next to me. I stroked his fur, taking comfort in his presence, and wondered why anyone would not want to own an animal. They just made life better.

"Alright, baby girl, I've got food," a voice called and I raised my head to smile at Beau.

"Beau! Shouldn't you be working?"

"What's the point in owning the place if I can't take off a night or two?" Beau said cheerfully, but I could read the worry lines in his face. His style was on point today with a loose linen button-down tucked lightly into faded seersucker shorts, his ancient topsiders on his feet.

"You heard."

"I did. And I'm coming to support you and keep

anyone away from your house that you don't want here," Beau said, easing a platter covered with tin foil onto the table.

"You brought food. I could kiss you," I said and did just that when he plopped beside me to wrap his arms around me.

"It's going to get ugly," Beau said against my ear, referring to the town gossip.

"How bad is it?" I said, drawing back to study his face.

"Well, details are slowly trickling in. First we heard drowned body. Then we heard murder. Later on, suspicion was put on you and Trace."

I gasped.

"Chief Dupree!" I spit out. "That bastard was trying to pin it on us when we were on the boat."

"Well, that yummy Coast Guard Petty something or other set us all straight pretty quickly on that one. You should've seen Dupree's face when he contradicted that silly story. So, it seems we all know Renaldo was murdered and that you and Trace found the body."

"You were there? How's Trace?" I asked, guilt rushing through me as I thought about him dealing with the horde of gossips at the wharf.

"Trace is fine," a voice said and I started as Luna and Trace came out onto the porch. Hank jumped up and wiggled over to Trace, one of his favorite people.

"Oh God, Trace, I'm sorry I left you. I had to tell Luna," I said.

"I know, I told you to go."

"Was it bad?"

"Besides me almost punching an officer of the law? It

was typical small-town excitement," Trace said, plopping down in a chair across from me. His face showed the strain of the day and I felt more connected to him for what we had been through as a team.

"Thanks, Trace. You saved me today," I said, meeting his eyes, feeling heat rush through me as he held my gaze.

"You held your own. I'm really impressed," Trace said.

I blushed a little, enjoying the compliment from him.

"Hmm," Beau said, looking between us.

The doorbell rang.

"I'll handle this," Beau said, popping up.

The three of us stayed silent as we strained to hear who was at the door.

"Well, bless your heart, that's so kind of you to think of her. I'll be sure to let her know you stopped by," Beau said as he closed the door on a protesting voice. The bell rang again but Beau ignored it, coming out to the patio again.

"Press," Beau said easily.

"Shit," I groaned.

"'No comment' is all you say. This is a police investigation," Beau observed.

"They aren't going to leave us alone," I said.

"Well, you are just going to make them wait then, honey," Beau said, coming back onto the porch with a stack of plates and a handful of cutlery. "Now, dig in. Y'all look like shriveled up balloons, wilting all over the place. Eat, eat."

It felt weird to eat, after finding a dead body, but I couldn't deny that I was hungry. I held out my hand for a plate and Beau gave me an approving nod as he dished up some blackened chicken and roasted vegetables with a side of rice. Not saying a word, I began to eat, closing my eyes in pleasure as the flavors assaulted my tongue.

"Sorry, Luna. Althea told me that you had just gone on a date with him," Trace said and Beau's head swung around, scenting gossip.

"You did? Well, all sorts of romances firing up this week," he said and then winced, probably realizing that one romance wouldn't be taking off. "Sorry, Luna."

"Thanks, guys. I'm still kind of absorbing the news. It's even more shocking to realize it was a murder."

"When did you last see him?" Trace asked and Luna blushed, quickly shoving a piece of chicken in her mouth.

"Oh." Beau nodded knowingly.

"Aside from, ahem, all that." Trace waved away Luna's night of passion. "Like when did you see him last?"

"When I left the boat. We made plans to have dinner this weekend and he said he would call me later that day. And then…nothing. I was so pissed at him too," Luna said, stabbing a pepper with her fork.

"Understandably," Beau said soothingly.

"So this was when?"

"Thursday morning."

"It must've happened shortly after, because the body's been in the water long enough to have the fish eat some of it," Trace mused.

Luna's fork clattered to her plate as she pushed her food away and marched into the living room. Beau immediately jumped up and shot a withering gaze at Trace.

"Sorry, I wasn't thinking," Trace said on a sigh, running his hands through his hair, shame etched across his face.

"It's okay. We're all a little in shock at the moment," I said.

"How are you holding up?" Trace asked, leaning back to scan my face again.

"Could be better. Stopped by Miss Elva's and had a nice cry. She said it's going to get worse before it gets better."

Trace raised an eyebrow at me.

"Hey, don't knock it. She was right about today."

"Do you see anything?"

"Honestly, I haven't tried. I'm pretty wiped out. I think I'll get some sleep tonight and try to center myself in the morning, come at this fresh," I said, glossing over what I had encountered on the docks. More than half the town had been clustered on the dock; it would be somewhat impossible to pick out who had been giving off that vibe.

A knock at the door had me starting to get up, but Beau called to me to sit. I sat, nibbling on my lip in worry as I tried to sift through the impressions I had received on the dock after we had gotten off the boat.

"I'm going to stay here tonight," Trace said, his voice firm.

"Actually, I'm going to stay," a commanding voice said from the doorway and I swear my skin got goose bumps.

"What makes you think that?" Trace said, standing up to square off to Cash. Beau slipped quickly past the two and slid onto the couch next to me, snagging the tequila bottle in one hand.

"Drinks for the entertainment," he whispered to me and poured a healthy dose of the clear liquid into my glass.

Despite it all, I snorted at Beau, trying to contain my laughter.

"Because I've worked in security and I'm comfortable with keeping Althea safe," Cash said evenly, crossing his arms over his chest, his biceps rippling under the gray t-shirt he wore.

"Oh my," Beau whispered, admiring the view.

"I know, I can't even…" I whispered back.

"I can keep Althea safe," Trace shot back, crossing his arms across his chest to mirror Cash's pose. Though Trace's muscles were smaller, both men looked capable of hand-to-hand combat. As I thought more about hand-to-hand, my mind drifted into naughty places that I shouldn't be thinking about when two men were about to fight right in front of me.

"Is that so? How many intruders have you fought off? Are you armed? What do you carry?" Cash said evenly, his eyes never leaving Trace's face.

"It's time for you to leave," Trace said, ignoring Cash's questions.

"That's not for you to say," Cash said and turned to slide his gaze over me. I shivered just looking at him and tamped down on my inner-slut that wanted to have him protect me all night long.

"I believe it is, mate," Trace said softly, stepping into Cash's personal space. Beau and I both drew in a breath and I immediately jumped up.

"Okay, guys, it's been a tough day all around. Cash, thank you for coming, but I don't want to see you and Trace fight right now," I said, walking over to where Cash stood, easing myself between him and Trace. Running my hands over his bicep until I reached his hand, I tugged a bit, pulling him to follow me into the kitchen and away from Trace. I shook my head at Luna, who was sitting on a stool at the kitchen counter. Taking my cue, she got up and went out to the porch, leaving Cash and me alone.

"That guy," Cash said, shaking his head about Trace.

"Sorry about that, he's a little protective of me," I said softly, meeting his eyes, trying desperately to get a read on him. I just couldn't fathom Cash being a killer.

"You should have told me if you were dating someone," Cash said, and I finally caught the undercurrent of anger in his voice.

"I…I'm not," I said, reaching up to put my hand to his face, but he stepped back out of my reach.

"Sure looks like it to me," he bit out.

"It's nothing. We've just been good friends for a long time," I rushed out, pleading with him to understand.

"I don't poach. And I never cheat. So this shit doesn't fly with me," Cash said, moving towards the door. "I came here tonight to see if you were okay and to offer to protect you, not to find out that you were already involved."

"Cash, wait, I swear it's not what you think," I said, stopping him before he could walk out the door.

"Then you need to set lover boy straight, because he has a serious crush on you," Cash said, looking down at me.

"I…I don't even know. He's never been like that before," I whispered and I saw the tension ease in Cash's eyes a bit.

"Be careful. You don't know who the killer is and for all we know, you, or Luna…or any one of us could be the next target. Don't be alone. Close the blinds. Lock the doors."

"Do you really think he'd come after us?"

"Or she," Cash said.

"Shit, or she?"

"Yes, I think anything's possible. Especially if they think you and Trace had any sort of clues as to who they are…" Cash trailed off and sighed.

Tipping his head down, he bumped his forehead against mine before taking a nip of my bottom lip. Warmth surged through my body and I gasped a bit for air, feeling a bit dizzy as I leaned into his strength.

"Watch your back," he said and opened the door, slipping out quickly but giving me enough time to see the line of people with cameras that stood outside my door. Slamming the door on the shouted questions, I leaned my forehead against the wood for a second before taking a deep breath and turning, ready to return to my friends.

And briefly wondering if I had just exchanged a kiss with the killer.

Chapter Sixteen

HOURS LATER, I hiccupped as I watched Trace stroke Hank's back, the dog having wiggled his way up until his head rested on Trace's knee.

"Luna go to bed?" Trace asked.

"Yeah, she was done. I tucked her into one of the guestrooms."

"I can take a couch down here," Trace said.

"You don't have to stay, Trace. I'm sure it's fine."

"I'm staying. At least for the night, until we see what else the police come up with in the morning,"

I rolled my head to the side, resting against the back of the couch, and looked at Trace. He had taken on a bit of a glow for me – but that was probably due in large part to the amount of tequila I had imbibed this evening. Everything seemed a little softer around the edges, and with my shields down, Trace's aura glowed gently around him.

"You're glowing," I giggled and he squinted at me.

"Althea Rose, I do believe you are drunk," he said on a smile and stood, gently dislodging Hank from his legs. I smiled up at him as he came to stand before me, bending down to grab my arms and pull me to my feet.

"Whoa," I said as I wobbled into him, brushing against his body and feeling a languid heat curl through me at his nearness.

"This way, Tequila Thea," Trace said and I giggled again as he pulled me from the patio, stopping to lock and secure the doors, Hank two steps ahead of us. I watched as Trace walked around to all of the windows, checking that each was locked, pulling blinds tightly closed.

"Thank you," I said.

"No problem. Go on up, I'll crash down here."

"I have a second guest bedroom," I said, pausing at the stairs to watch him as Hank stood between us, his head swinging to look at each person speaking.

"I'll feel better being down here. Just in case," Trace said.

"Okay, come help with pillows and blankets then," I said, knowing I'd probably trip on a blanket and take a header down the stairs if I tried to walk back down with my arms full.

"Yes, ma'am," Trace said, his voice right behind me as we ascended the stairs and I felt myself grow warm at the thought of Trace bypassing the closet and following me into my bedroom.

One long narrow hallway shot to the back of the house with various doorways along the way, and a warm glow spilled from a small light in my bedroom, softly illuminating the hallway.

"Oof," Trace said as he bumped into me when I paused in front of the linen closet.

"Sorry," I whispered and moved to pull the linen closet open.

Hands at my waist stopped me, and I took a slow breath in, unsure of what was about to happen.

"I just want one," Trace whispered, his breath hot at my neck, causing me to shiver again.

"One what?" I whispered, closing my eyes as his lips brushed a sensitive spot on the back of my neck.

Trace slowly turned me until I was looking at his chest.

"Look at me," he whispered and I did, his eyes gleaming in the semi-darkness. My mouth went dry and I swallowed, waiting.

"One kiss. I know you've got something with Cash, but I just have to see," Trace said, and bent, nibbling softly at my bottom lip before I could offer a protest.

I surprised even myself when I leaned in, running my hands up his arms and through his hair, pulling his face to mine in an epic *I'm drunk and shouldn't be doing this but it feels so good* kiss.

We broke apart, both of us panting a little, and my heart banged an unsteady rhythm against my chest.

"You don't get to blame this on being drunk," Trace said, leaning in to brush his lips softly against mine again.

"Shit," I said, my hands curling into his shirt.

"I just had to know."

"Know what?"

"I had to know if it's there."

"Is it?" I asked, mentally wanting to kick myself for going down this road.

Trace just smiled and stepped back, running a finger down my nose.

"Sleep tight," he said, turning to walk down the hallway.

"Wait," I said and he turned, a smile lighting his face.

"Your blankets," I mumbled and the smile dropped, but he nodded.

"Thanks," he said, grabbing them from me and moving down the hallway. Hank followed him, standing at the top of the stairs and looking down before looking back at me.

"You can go with him," I said, though I knew I would miss his warm comfort in my bed.

With a grunt, Hank turned from the stairs and followed me into my room.

I couldn't help but smile even though I wondered if I would be able to sleep with all the thoughts whirling through my head.

But for now, Hank was the only man that needed to be in my bed.

Chapter Seventeen

I WOKE UP to a dull pounding at the door.

Or was it in my head? My brain felt fuzzy as I squinted my eyes open to see Hank standing at the end of my bed, his head cocked at the door.

"Come in?" I asked, not sure if I had really heard the pounding or not.

"Morning, sunshine," Luna sang, swinging into my room with a wine glass full of orange juice. Hank bounced around at the end of the bed, wanting attention.

"Is that orange juice?"

"Mimosa. Just enough to take the edge off without dulling your senses," she said, smiling at me as she eased down onto the bed.

"You're an angel," I said, grabbing the glass and gulping half of it down before I put it on the bedside stand.

"You don't look so good," Luna observed and I laughed, pushing my hair back from my face.

"I went about three tequilas past where I should've last night," I said sheepishly.

Luna glanced to where the door stood open and got up to close it quickly before settling back onto my bed. I sighed, knowing girl talk was coming.

"So, what the hell is going on with you and Trace? And you and Cash?"

"I wish I knew the answers to that," I said, my eyes roaming to a crystal light catcher in butterfly shapes hanging in my window.

"I mean…Cash is crazy hot and I think you should ride that train as long as you can. But Trace was a surprise. I had no idea there was a history there."

I sliced my eyes back to hers. "There wasn't."

"Wasn't?" Luna's voice went up a note.

"We kissed. By the closet, last night, blankets," I mumbled, burying my face in my glass again.

"You kissed him?" Luna squealed.

"Shhhh," I said.

"Shhh what? Like he doesn't know you guys kissed?" Luna demanded.

"Well, maybe I don't want him to know we are discussing it," I hissed at her.

"How was it?" she whispered, excitement covering her face.

"Amazing," I admitted, looking gloomily into my drink.

"So why the face?" Luna asked, stroking Hank's tummy as he wiggled on his back on the bed in delight.

I shrugged, looking away from her as I bit my lip, surprised when tears spiked my eyes.

"Whoa, what's wrong, honey?" Luna asked, her mouth dropping open.

"It's just that…for once I found a really great guy. And he took me on a nice date and he has a mouth that I could kiss for hours and I really want to see where it'll go with him."

"But?"

"But, now this Trace thing came out of nowhere and he's like, moving in on my space, and I don't know what to do because I like him too," I said, softly, as I stared at the wall.

"Shitty timing," Luna said.

"Yeah, really shitty," I said, turning to look at her. "I just never meet guys like this and now I have two and knowing me, this is going to all blow up in my face in a fiery catastrophe that leaves me single and collecting cats."

Hank tilted his head at me and I laughed.

"Or dogs. Collecting more dogs."

"It will all work out. I promise. One thing I learned about dating more than one guy at a time? Always be very honest and open about your intentions. That way you don't come off as though you are trying to hide something," Luna said.

I flashed back to Cash's anger from the night before. He had obviously picked up on the Trace thing and felt like I was hiding it from him.

"Cash thinks I've been lying to him about Trace."

"Well, you'll need to set him straight then. If that's what you want."

"The only thing I want right now is to get rid of this headache. Then we need to do a seeing spell," I said, meeting Luna's eyes.

"What are we trying to see exactly?" Luna said, her eyebrows raised in question.

"I want to see if we can find out who the killer is."

Luna blew out a breath and pushed her bangs back from her eyes.

"Don't you think we should leave this to the police?"

"Is that what you want to do?" I asked incredulously, thinking about how Dupree had tried to incriminate us yesterday.

Luna's lips pressed together in a thin line as she shook her head.

"No. No, I really don't. Okay, let's head to the shop."

"I need to shower first."

Luna wrinkled her nose at me and nodded.

"Come on, Hank, I bet you're hungry. Your slut of a mom needs to shower," she said as she got off the bed.

My pillow just missed hitting her on the way out the door.

Chapter Eighteen

"WHAT EXACTLY ARE we doing here again?" Trace asked impatiently as we unlocked the door to our store.

"You didn't have to come, you know," I said over my shoulder before I pushed into the shop, immediately moving to the windows and pulling the blinds down to discourage onlookers.

We'd narrowly avoided being run down by the press this morning, by sending Trace out as a decoy. He'd managed to shake them after a mile or so and had arrived at the shop just as we were unlocking the door.

"Yeah, like I'm going to leave you guys alone," Trace scoffed, his manhood offended.

" I hope you like witchcraft, then, because we are about to do a seeing spell. Well, I should say Luna's going to use her magic and I'm going to harness my gift. Together, we should be able to figure a few things out."

"Magic?" Trace said, and looked like he was going to say something further but then he stopped.

"Yes, I'm a white witch. For reasons that I am sure you

are aware of, I like to keep that fact under the radar," Luna said smoothly, smiling her most charming smile at Trace. He couldn't help but smile back and I shook my head at them both. When Luna turned up the charm, nobody could resist.

"Of course, Luna. I'd never say anything," Trace said easily and I wondered briefly if Luna had actually charmed him – in the magical sense, that is.

"Good. It's just a little bit of white magic. We'll just poke around a bit and see if anything pops up in regards to Renaldo's murder," Luna said soothingly as she moved to the back of the room where a locked chest of drawers stood. No ugly steel file cabinet on display for Luna – instead she concealed the locked set of drawers inside a pretty reclaimed-wood armoire. More than one client had asked if it was for sale.

I watched Trace carefully to see if he had any reaction to Luna's revelation about being a witch. Because if he did, well, he would be off my list for me. Luna and I were a package deal, I thought as I moved towards the back of the shop.

Luna's presence this morning had helped us to gloss over any awkwardness about the night before and as far as I was concerned, the kiss had never happened.

"What's the purpose of a seeing spell?" Trace asked, leaning against the counter where the register stood. He wore yesterday's clothes, though I knew he had showered this morning. His blond hair was tucked back in its customary small ponytail and I wanted to tug on it a bit, to let his hair flow out.

"Althea," Luna warned and I pulled my thoughts away from Trace.

"Yes? Sorry?"

"Trace would like to know what the purpose of this seeing spell is," she said, refocusing on the items she was pulling from her shelves.

"Um, I think for this particular spell, we should focus on being able to see through illusions," I said as I tapped my finger against my mouth, considering all options for seeing spells that we could use.

"Agreed," Luna said and then turned, gesturing for us to follow her into her back room.

"Trippy," Trace observed, standing at the doorway of Luna's workshop. The wooden floors were clean and a circle of protection was chalked on the floor. Enormous crystals of various shapes and sizes lined the walls of the room, each to be used in different spell castings. A small altar held various mortar and pestle sets along with a variety of other tools used in spell casting.

Luna moved to the circle and bent to place white candles at interval points around the circle. In the middle, she placed a shallow clear glass bowl of water and poured a few drops of liquid from an amber bottle into the bowl.

"Sit," Luna said and Trace and I moved into the room, sitting at equal points around the circle so that we formed a triangle within the circle.

"What's going to happen?" Trace whispered.

"You're going to not talk," I said adamantly and then clamped down on a snort when he stuck his tongue out at me.

"Children. Knock it off," Luna said and closed her eyes, signaling for us to do the same.

Closing my eyes, I did my best to clear my mind of any thoughts, and just focused on my breath as I waited for Luna's incantation.

"Angels of future, Angels of past,
   Make my magic strong to last
   Through this water
   Show me the truth

What I want to see
   I'll finally find
   What I try to foresee
   Will be shown in my mind."

I kept my eyes closed as Luna leaned over to stir the contents of the bowl and instead, focused on any sort of vision that would arise for me.

"Drink," Luna said and I popped my eyes open to see her handing me the bowl of water. Reaching out, I brought the bowl to my lips, drinking the cool liquid and hoping this magic would work.

"Now we wait," Luna said and Trace looked like he was going to open his mouth, but I shook my head before closing my eyes. Pulling deep breaths through my nose, I let my mind clear as I focused my internal gaze on the third eye point in my forehead, allowing myself to drift into a slightly meditative state.

A poof of white clouds materialized and then, as though a strong wind blew them, they disappeared to show me the interior of Luca's Deli Shop. My breath caught as my view turned to see Theodore and Cash ordering at the counter. Luca, every bit the New Jersey Italian with a gold chain and velour tracksuit on, joked with them behind the deli counter as he prepared their sandwiches. The men laughed together, sharing a joke, as my heart got caught in my throat and I realized that one of them was a murderer.

"Open up!" A voice from outside the shop interrupted our spell.

I jerked my eyes open and shook my head to clear my thoughts, a wave of dizziness washing over me as I watched Trace stand up and send a questioning glance to Luna.

"Yes, it's fine. Go see who it is," she murmured, bending over to blow out the candles and put the dish on her altar. Straightening, she smoothed her linen shift dress and met my eyes.

"This isn't going to be good," Luna said, nodding towards the front door.

"Why?"

"I saw it. In my vision. What did you see?"

"Luca's Deli. Cash and Theodore were chatting with Luca as they ordered sandwiches."

Luna grimaced and shook her head.

"It can't be Cash."

"We don't know that," I whispered, glancing towards where low voices rumbled through the door.

"Listen, take my key to my cabinet. There's a spell book in there that you will need," Luna whispered, stepping forward to press a small key into my palm. Panic fluttered through my stomach as I saw the fear in her eyes.

"Luna, what's happening?"

Luna just shook her head at me, indicating that I should stop talking, and moved into the front room. Slipping the key into the pocket of my linen pants, I followed her, nerves making me chew at my bottom lip.

"Ah, there she is," Chief Dupree said, all but singing the words out as he came into the shop. If he could have puffed out his chest any further he would've looked just like the rooster down on County A.

"Officer Dupree," I said, assuming he was speaking to me.

"Ms. Rose, that's Chief Dupree," he corrected and then turned to Luna. The hair on the back of my neck stood up as it flashed to me what he was about to do.

"No," I said, moving to stand in front of Luna.

"It's okay, Althea, he's just doing his job," Luna said, running a hand softly down my back.

"No, this is wrong," I said, staring down Chief Dupree and enunciating my words very carefully, as though he was hard of hearing.

"I'm sorry but I have to take your friend in for questioning, as she was the last person to see the deceased," Chief Dupree said, a smirk on his face.

"This is ridiculous," I said, "You can ask her questions right here."

Chief Dupree looked around, a sneer on his face as he took in the crystals and healing elixirs.

"Luna Lavelle, I need to take you in for questioning on the murder of Renaldo Santiago," Chief Dupree said, reaching for his handcuffs.

"Wait just a minute," I said, moving to stand even closer to Chief Dupree so that we were eye to eye.

"Careful, Ms. Rose," he drawled, his chin coming up as he met my eyes.

"From my understanding of the law, which I am certain you have studied at some point, yes?, you need to charge her with a crime before you put her in handcuffs. Asking her to come down to the station to answer questions certainly doesn't require aggressive force on your part, does it now?" I said, heavy on the sarcasm.

Chief Dupree's face flushed and if he could have spat on me, I swear he would have.

"Now, Ms. Rose, there's no need for handcuffs. Ms. Lavelle? Will you willingly come with me to the station to answer a few questions?"

"Don't go, Luna," I said, whipping my head around.

"Careful, Ms. Rose, or I'll slap you with an obstruction of justice charge," Chief Dupree drawled and my mouth dropped open. Stepping back, I raised my hands in the air.

"Looks like you've gone a little power hungry now that you have a real case to try. I'll be watching you very carefully, *Officer* Dupree. Don't think I can't pull out the big guns if you step one inch out of line with Luna," I threatened, and Trace came to stand beside me, wrapping his arm around my shoulder in support.

Chief Dupree looked a little white around the gills and he nodded, understanding my intent.

"It's going to be okay," Luna whispered, leaning in to

wrap her arms around me. "In the safe...there's money. Use it if you need it. Don't forget the spell book. The breaking spell. Towards the back."

"Enough chatter, ladies!" Chief Dupree barked and Luna straightened, giving me a quick kiss on the cheek.

"Call me when you are done, we'll come pick you up," I said, not even bothering to address Dupree as he led Luna from the shop. The blinds were still closed, which spared me the sight of seeing beautiful Luna being put into the back seat of the cop car.

Whirling, I grabbed Trace's arms.

"We need to get Beau. This is going to be bad."

"What do you think will happen?" Trace asked in surprise.

"Luna said it would be bad. She already knew. They are going to charge her with murder."

Chapter Nineteen

"YOU REALLY THINK they'll charge her?" Beau asked as he paced behind the warm teak wood of his bar, tossing a shaker back and forth between his hands. We'd come here directly from the shop, knowing that Lucky's wouldn't be open until 4:00 on a Sunday. Beau had met us at the door, ushering us in and locking it after us.

"There's no reason to. But Luna knew something bad was about to go down."

"We have to solve this before they get too far," Beau said, coming to stand in front of me and holding up a bottle of vodka.

"No, I need food," I said, waving away the drinks.

"Something from here? Or Luca's?"

Remembering the vision that had surfaced for me earlier, I considered going to Luca's to scope things out and see if I got any feelings.

"What are the chances of me walking down there and getting back without being hounded by the gossips or trapped by the press?"

"Zero," Trace said, rolling his eyes in disgust at the annoyances of living in a small town.

"I'll go. I eat here every day. Orders?" Beau asked and I smiled at him, loving him and all that he was.

"Turkey on rye," Trace and I both said at the same time and I blushed, looking away from the knowing look that crossed Beau's face.

"Oh, and pickles," I called after him.

"Duh," Beau called back and I smiled, though my nerves were clawing at me.

"When do you think we'll hear from her?"

"I don't know," Trace said, shaking his head and reaching down to pull his MacBook Air from his messenger bag.

"What are you doing?"

"I think we need to learn more about Renaldo."

Twenty minutes later, Beau returned with sandwiches and a grim look on his face while I hung over Trace's shoulder and took notes on what he found.

"This town is nuts," Beau declared, dropping onto a stool next to me and sliding the bag of food my way.

"You hadn't noticed?"

"No, like really nuts. Luca and his buddies are taking bets on who the murderer is."

"Shut up," I said, stopping as I burrowed into the brown paper bag, my stomach already growling at the thought of Luca's turkey sandwich.

"It's like – I love this town – and then they go and pull some crazy shit like that," Trace murmured, his eyes still focused on the computer.

"Who's favored?" I asked, deciding if you can't beat

'em, join 'em. I pulled wax paper-wrapped sandwiches from the bag and handed them off, along with sea salt potato chips and the best pickles you'll find this side of New Jersey.

"Luna's leading," Beau said gravely and my mouth dropped open.

"How do they know that?"

"Seems like Dupree stopped by the deli for a chat before he headed on in to pull Luna in for questioning," Beau said, taking a small bite of his sandwich.

"Can he even do that? Is that even legal? He'll smear her name in this town. That's slander!" I said, slamming my hand onto the bar so hard that Trace's computer shook.

"Dupree does what he wants," Trace said.

"There has to be a way to stop this," I moaned.

"There is. Solve the murder," Beau observed and I sighed, knowing he was right.

"Do you have your laptop here? We've been trying to gather information on Renaldo," I said.

"Cash would be a great help with this – he used to work in security, you know," Beau said as he strode across the restaurant to step into his office.

"That guy," Trace said, disdain in his voice.

"He may be right though; I bet Cash could dig a little deeper than we could," I said, immediately stuffing the sandwich in my mouth to stop any other words that would most likely piss Trace off.

"I've been known to dabble in some hacking. Let me see what I can do first before you call lover boy," Trace said.

"Oh? What about shy Sienna? Didn't you miss out on a

date last night with her?" I said, and then clamped my mouth shut and counted to ten.

"Children, knock it off," Beau ordered.

Trace just shook his head at me and went back to his computer.

"What was Renaldo's job exactly?" Beau asked, coming to sit next to us again, his laptop in hand.

"I know that Cash said he worked with some investors. I believe it was maybe a competing group? I'm not totally sure..." I trailed off when I saw Trace's face go stony with the mention of Cash's name again. When he finally looked up at me, I just shook my head at him. Now was *so* not the time for jealousy.

"He was a consultant, from what I understand," Beau said, taking a bite from his sandwich and tapping at his keyboard to pull up Google.

"I hate that word – consultant. It sounds so mobbish," I said, rolling my eyes.

"Or like someone who was made redundant at his company and went out on his own," Trace said.

"I suppose," I said, not willing to give Renaldo – may he rest in peace – the benefit of the doubt. As far as I was concerned, people didn't end up with an anchor attached to their legs when they were walking the straight and narrow. There was something we were missing and I highly doubted that Renaldo would turn out to be a squeaky clean investor who was in town for new opportunities.

"Okay, so I am finding a Renaldo – from Puerto Rico. It looks like he was working for a company called S&L Investments. A search on S&L investments turns up literally nothing, not even a web page. It's like they don't even exist."

"Could be a fake name," Beau supplied and I nodded.

"Maybe he just made the name up and was here on some other mission."

"Although I do know that we are in competition with another investment group for Luca's space," Beau said as he reached for a pickle.

"You think that group is S&L?"

"I think Cash would have the answer to that," Beau said, turning to raise an eyebrow at me and I gulped as my mouth went dry.

"What if Cash is involved?" I whispered, staring down at my sandwich, hating that I had to throw him into the line of fire. There was little I could do though – my best friend was being held by a maniac of a police chief.

"Why do you say that?" Beau said with a gasp, swinging towards me.

Trace snorted, a pleased smile crossing his face.

"That guy," he said again.

"Knock it off, Trace," I warned.

"You didn't see something, did you?" Beau asked, tugging on my hand to pull my attention back to him.

"We were in the middle of a seeing spell earlier today," I began, not having to explain to Beau what Luna was. There were no secrets between the three of us. "And before Dupree came and interrupted us, I saw Theodore and Cash talking."

"The spell was to dissolve illusions – to make you see who's lying," Trace said cheerfully.

"So either Cash or Theodore is lying to us?"

"Or both!" Trace said happily.

"Trace! That's it! Cash is a nice guy and I happen to care about him so I would really appreciate it if you'd show some humility and just knock it off."

"You're really a piece of work, Althea," Trace said, slamming his laptop closed and shoving back from the bar.

"Trace, just stop. There's a lot going on right now. I don't need some pissing match between you and Cash – if they charge Luna, it's on us to save her," I said, refusing to back down.

"And while you try to play nice, you may be sleeping with a murderer," Trace hissed in my face before storming across the dining room towards the patio.

"I'm not sleeping with him," I shouted, the slamming of the door my only answer.

"Well, then," Beau said, fanning his face dramatically. "I swear, if we didn't have a murder to solve, I'd mix up a cocktail and watch the sparks from this little drama."

"Ugh, Beau, what am I going to do?" I said, burying my face in my hands.

"Well, sweetie, you're going to put your big girl panties on and solve a murder," Beau said sweetly and I pulled back to glare at him.

"How? I can't even work with the two men who could actually be of some help."

Beau pulled back and raised an eyebrow at me. "And what do you think I am?"

"Sorry, Beau, of course you can help. I just know how busy you are with the restaurant."

"Well, I'll close it for a day or two. No big deal," Beau said and picked up his cell phone to start calling his staff.

When I grabbed his arm to stop him, he just shook me off. Covering the mouthpiece, he shushed me.

"You and Luna are my best friends. If you think I can't close the restaurant for a few days until we figure this out then you had better reexamine your definition of friendship," he sniffed, clearly offended.

Nodding, I blew out a breath and tugged my hair back. I suspected we were about to walk into a tornado.

Chapter Twenty

AN HOUR LATER, my phone trilled from where it sat on the bar and I jumped, knocking my funny bone against the corner of the stool.

"Ow, ow, ow," I cursed, reaching to glance at the screen. "I don't know this number."

"Just answer it," Beau said from where he sat, scrolling through his laptop. Trace hadn't come back after his little snit; as far as I was concerned, he could stay out on the patio or wherever the heck he had gone. It wasn't worth my time right now to hold his hand.

"Hello?" I answered, leaning back against the bar and meeting Beau's eyes.

"Ms. Rose?" Chief Dupree's sugarcoated drawl reached me through the phone and I felt the hair on the back of my neck rise.

"Yes, I'm assuming this is Officer Dupree?" I asked sweetly.

"That's *Chief* Dupree to you, Ms. Rose, and I'll ask you not to forget it again."

"Sorry, Officer," I said again and saw Beau shake his head at me.

"I'm calling to inform you that Ms. Lavelle is being charged with the murder of Renaldo Santiago."

"That was quick. Doesn't take you long to frame someone, does it now, Officer?" I seethed into the phone, my hand gripping it so tightly that I'm surprised it didn't shatter.

"Be careful, Ms. Rose, threatening an officer of the law can land you right next to your little friend in here."

"Oh, so *now* you're an officer? Please. I didn't threaten you and we both know it. Just like we know that Luna didn't murder Renaldo. I'll have her out on bail tomorrow and don't think I won't be suing you for slander for your little chat down at Luca's before you even went to question Luna. My mother has some of the best lawyers in the nation on call."

I didn't like using my mother's contacts that often, but when Luna's life was on the line? I would use everything I had to save her.

"I'm sure that won't be necessary," Chief Dupree said, "and, you'll need to wait until Wednesday for a bail hearing as the judge won't be back from his vacation to the Caymans until then."

"What!" I screeched, pulling the phone away to look at it in disbelief. Beau rose from the table, walking towards me quickly, a question on his face.

"I'm sorry, Ms. Rose, there's nothing that can be done."

"You are violating her rights, Dupree. The Caymans are less than a two-hour flight away, so bring that judge back now. If she doesn't get a bail hearing by Tuesday at the latest, I will hunt you down and make your life a living hell, so full of legal red tape that you'll wish that you never signed on to be a police officer in little Tequila Key. You're entering a world of pain, *Officer*," I swore as I turned my phone off on his protesting words, knowing that I literally couldn't stand hearing his voice anymore or I would scream.

"What's happening?" Beau asked, wrapping his arm around me. Trembling wracked my body and I leaned into Beau for a moment, needing his strength.

"They've charged her with murder and they say she can't get a bail hearing until at least Wednesday because the judge is on vacation."

"Is that even legal? They can't just keep her there," Beau protested.

"It appears they can. I need to get a hold of my mother," I said, hating to think about Luna, such an elegant and classy woman, being held in the dumpy little jail downtown.

"Why don't you go get Trace first?" Beau asked gently and I raised my eyebrow at him.

"What? You want me to apologize? It's not my job to placate him right now. It's not like we are even dating," I said, putting my hands at my hips.

"Kindness never goes out of style, my friend," Beau said, running a finger down my nose. "Now, go. I'll email your mother."

Dang it. Why did Beau always have to be right about everything? Gnawing on my lip again, I made my way towards the patio, trying my best not to stomp my feet like I wanted to.

Easing the door open, I poked my head out to see Trace stretched out on a lounge chair, his eyes on the ocean that stretched before us.

"Hey," I said softly, moving across the patio to drop onto the chair next to him.

"Hey," he said back, his eyes never leaving the ocean.

"Listen, I'm sorry if I hurt your feelings. It's just…a lot right now. I don't think that I can handle all of these extra…things." I waved my hand in the air lamely, trying to think of a better word to encompass everything that had evolved between the men in my life and myself in a matter of days.

"I get it," Trace said stiffly, still staring out at the ocean, the picture of a wounded puppy that had just been kicked.

"Trace!" I said sharply and he jumped, glancing at me in surprise.

"I'm not rejecting you. I'm not saying yes and I'm not saying no. I'm just saying not right now!" I all but shouted, and then forced myself to bring my decibel level down.

Inside voices, I lectured myself in my head.

Trace held up his hands, but a smile flitted across his face briefly. "Okay, okay. Loud and clear."

I breathed a sigh of relief.

"Thank you. Because Luna just got charged with murder and Dupree isn't letting her get a bail hearing until at least Wednesday. We need to solve this like yesterday," I said, turning to scan my eyes along the beach below us. A glint of light reflecting off of something caught my eye and I saw a flash of red.

"Trace, let's go inside. Now. I think someone is taking

pictures of us," I breathed, smiling and nodding at Trace like an idiot to pretend like I hadn't just seen a reflection off the lens of a camera.

"Damn paparazzi," Trace seethed, slamming his laptop closed and following me across the patio into the restaurant.

"Paparazzi? We're not famous. And Tequila Key doesn't have paparazzi," I said, surprised when a high-pitched giggle whistled from my throat. Biting down my lips, I realized that I was dangerously close to having a serious giggle fit.

"Oh God," Trace said, scanning my face before motioning to Beau.

"Whiskey. She needs a shot of whiskey," he called and Beau nodded, jumping behind the bar to pour me some-thing from a bottle that I couldn't see. I had started to huff and puff in an effort to keep the giggles down, but the more that I did, the more they threatened to bubble up. I was like a kid in Sunday mass, and there was no stopping this train.

"Drink," Beau ordered, sliding the shot glass down the bar in an amazing *Cocktail*-like move. I snagged it before it could slide off the end and slammed it down, the sheer fire of it causing my giggles to come to an abrupt stop.

"Thank you," I gasped, sputtering against the burn in my throat.

"You can't lose it on us. There just ain't time for any of that nonsense, honey," Beau said.

"God, you're so right," I breathed, sliding onto a stool and putting my head in my hands.

"Althea, you have to see what you can do to tap into your second sight again," Trace said, sitting beside me.

"The problem is – I'm exhausted and emotionally on edge. I never, ever, read well when I'm like that," I said. "You can't always trust what comes through."

Trace shot Beau a glance and Beau just shrugged.

"Okay, back to the old-fashioned way then," Trace said, pulling his laptop out.

"Follow the money," Beau quipped.

Trace didn't even look up from his computer, just forming his hand into a shooting motion at Beau. "Bull's-eye."

Chapter Twenty-One

AS NIGHT CREPT IN, I paced the restaurant, frustrated with the lack of momentum. Beau was at the door, having a conversation with what I assumed was another patron he was turning away. Guilt crept up my spine for a moment but then I shook it off, knowing that Beau loved Luna just as much as I did.

"Althea, it's Craig Donaldson," Beau called and I cringed.

Craig Donaldson was the local reporter for the weekly *Tequila Tales* newspaper. I grimaced, just thinking about how he would sensationalize this story. Murder was big news in any town, but in Tequila Key?

Luna had no chance.

"No comment," I called.

"He says if you talk to him, he promises to stop hounding you. Or I'll pull all the advertising from his paper," Beau said sweetly, though I could hear the steel ranging under his voice.

I had to laugh. If Beau pulled his advertising, the newspaper would struggle to stay open.

"Why don't you just pull your advertising then?" I said, just so I could stress Craig out as I slowly made my way to the door.

"Maybe I should," Beau mused, playing along.

"Because I'd hate for you to advertise at a paper that only prints lies. Seems as though that would be more of a tabloid, really," I said, coming to rest against the doorframe, running my eyes over Craig's now slightly panicked face. Mid-fifties and with a skin tone that was almost always one shade too pink, Craig could be your neighborhood accountant. He had never struck me as much of a reporter and I suspected that he was going to use this story to try and make his name.

"Craig," I said evenly, raising an eyebrow at him, noting that he was wearing a red shirt.

"Althea," Craig said, bobbing his head a little.

"Have fun taking pictures on the beach today?" I asked and Beau's chin came up as he looked down at Craig.

"Were you on my private beach-front property taking pictures today?" Beau asked and Craig shook his head vigorously.

"I was not," he said.

"Let's take a look," Beau said, snagging the camera strap that was slung over Craig's arm and ripping it from his body before Craig could do anything about it. My adoration of Beau went up even more as he single-handedly stiff-armed Craig while he scrolled through the pictures.

"Delete, delete, delete," Beau said, ruthlessly deleting all the images on the camera.

"You can't do that!" Craig cried.

"Looks like I just did. If I ever find you trespassing again, I'll sue you so fast you'll never be able to do business in this town again," Beau said softly and Craig's shoulders hunched as he nodded.

"I'm sorry. It's just such a big story and I couldn't get to Althea and Trace and they found the body and..." he sputtered. I raised a hand to cut him off.

"Listen up, you pipsqueak, if you even remotely suggest Luna is the murderer, I'll put a hex on you that will make your package shrink, if you get my meaning?" I said, using my reputation to help me for once.

Craig's face went white – well, the whitest I had ever seen it – and he nodded, gulping audibly.

"But what am I supposed to say about the murder then?"

"You say that we found a body and that the police are working on the case. You are only a weekly. Put the edition out tomorrow with those details," I ordered.

"But...but I know that Luna has been charged," he said.

"Well, just tell people you didn't know that by the time the print deadline came," I threatened.

"Can you give me any details about the body? Just something?" Craig pleaded and I sighed, running my hand through my hair again to tug at the ends.

"There was an anchor tied to the feet. You could see the claw marks on his legs where he had tried to get it off," I said, wincing as I thought back to Renaldo's bloated body. Craig scribbled in his notebook, nodding, switching into reporter mode.

"And how did you feel about finding him?" Craig asked, his eyes coming up to mine.

"How do you think I felt, Craig?" I asked, raising my eyebrow at him.

"I...I imagine you'd be pretty upset?" he asked.

"Yes, Craig. Upset, shocked, horrified. I'm lucky I didn't have a panic attack and die on the spot. Now, get out of here," I ordered.

Craig scurried down the walkway and I shook my head after him, turning to look up at Beau.

"Would you really pull your advertising?"

"Would you really be able to shrink his package?" he asked, a smirk crossing his face.

"Maybe. With Luna's help," I snorted, turning to go back inside, melancholy settling like a weight on my shoulders.

"On second thought, I'm going home. Hank needs me. Is there anything else we can do tonight?"

"No, but let me drive you," Beau insisted.

"I suppose I shouldn't turn down the offer," I sighed, calling to Trace.

"And you won't. I'm crashing with you tonight too, sugar."

"Do you think we can do this?" I rolled my head on the pillow to look at Beau an hour later. Hank snored softly at the end of the bed, worn out from running ecstatic circles when we had returned home, having first dropped Trace off at his house on the way. Trace had claimed that he wanted a change of clothes, but I think he just wanted to put some space between him and me.

"Solve a murder? No problem, sweetie. We just have to be extra diligent," Beau said.

"I'm worried about Luna. I wish they'd let me talk to her."

"Can you like...beam your thoughts into her head?" Beau asked and I raised an eyebrow at him.

"Beam my thoughts?"

"Whatever, I'm too tired to try and think of a politically correct term for the magic stuff you two do." Beau waved his hand at me and yawned, snuggling deeper into the covers.

"I don't know. I've never tried," I said, wondering if Luna and I could use our extra abilities to communicate.

"Just send her some love. Can you do that?"

"Yeah, I'll do that," I said, my eyes slipping closed as I imagined a big pulsing bright pink wave of light coming from the top of my head, floating over the town, and into the jail where Luna was. I waited for a moment, allowing the light to cover the jail, praying she could feel our love.

I gasped as a stunning white light – of course Luna's light was white – intense in its energy and beauty, met mine with such force that I knew it was Luna, my white witch best friend, telling me she was okay.

"She sends her love," I whispered, and Beau reached out to squeeze my hand.

"We'll kick some murderer-butt tomorrow," he promised.

Which was precisely what I was afraid of.

Chapter Twenty-Two

"I'M JUST GOING to get some things from the shop and then I'll meet you back here. Or do you want to go to your restaurant again?" I asked Beau, trying to change the subject from the fact that I was going off on my own for a bit.

"Meet back here so Hank can hang with us too," Beau decided, shrugging his shoulders in defeat.

"Hey, it'll be fine. I'll drop you off so you can grab clothes, pick up some sandwiches from Luca's, and be back to you within the hour. And frankly, why shouldn't I be worrying about you? Or Trace? Huh? Why do you seem to think they'll come after me?" I demanded, placing my hands on my hips and giving my best attitude to match my hot pink hair.

"Ugh, it's way too early for you to pull that out," Beau grumbled, walking to the front door.

I smiled after him, happy that I was getting my way.

"Hank! Toy!" I said, tossing a squeaky ball across the room as Beau and I stepped onto the porch and made our way to where my Mini was parked at the curb. Today was not a good day for beach cruisers.

Obviously.

"What do you want from Luca's?" I asked as I pulled away from the curb.

"Pastrami today, I think," Beau said, squinching up his cute face as he thought about it.

"Final answer?"

"No. Rotisserie chicken on wheat with that delightful avocado mayo he does," Beau decided.

"Okay. But he may spit in your food when I give him a piece of my mind about running bets on Luna," I said and saw Beau's grimace from the corner of my eye.

"Maybe you don't say anything about that until *after* he prepares the food? Just a thought?" Beau said as I pulled to a stop in front of his charming beach bungalow that made me sigh in envy every time I walked through it. It was like an HGTV reality show mixed with Martha Stewart had thrown up inside. It gave me something to aspire to, I suppose.

"Smooches," Beau called, hopping out of the car before turning to lean back in, his face moving into the shade.

"You get an hour before I send a search party."

"Yes, sir." I saluted him and gunned away from the curb as soon as he slammed the door. I needed to get Luna's spell book and make sure nothing else had been disturbed at the shop.

I'd had a fitful night of sleep after Luna's burst of light had reassured me that she was doing okay at the jail. Though I'd felt calmer about her safety, my questions about Cash had kept me up as I had nervously replayed the scene from the spell.

Cash or Theodore?

My bet was on Theodore. I just couldn't see Cash as a murderer.

As though he was reading my mind, my phone beeped with a text when I pulled up to the shop. Looking down at the screen as I unlocked the door, I stepped inside and leaned back against the door as I read the text.

Are you all right?

I couldn't help but feel a fluttery little squeeze around my heart at Cash's text. Moving to the back of the shop, I stopped in front of the armoire with Luna's safe.

Define all right, I texted back.

You haven't killed anyone? You're not locked up? All your delicious body parts are accounted for?

I shivered at his words, wondering just how his hands would feel on certain delicious body parts.

"Oh jeez," I said, quickly telling him I was just fine before turning to the safe to get Luna's spell book and some extra cash. I pulled the book – bound in supple white suede, naturally – from the safe and tucked it in my bag, along with a stack of cash, anticipating that I'd need to pay Luna's bond. I really hoped Dupree would let her have visitors today or at least have a phone call. I fully intended to go down to the station with Beau after lunch to harass Dupree's secretary into letting us talk to Luna.

The bells over the door sounded and I jumped, whipping around to see who had entered the shop.

Distracted by Cash's text, I had forgotten to lock the door.

"Theodore," I said, swallowing against the sudden dryness in my mouth. I didn't even need to drop my mental shields to feel the rush of anger that pulsed from his mind. A cheerful smile across his face belied his inner rage and I straightened, casting my eyes around for a weapon.

"Althea! Good to see you again," he called across the room, beginning to walk towards me.

"Theodore, cut the crap. I'm not happy with you after that little stunt you pulled when I was having dinner with Cash the other night. We're not open today so I'll have to ask you to leave," I said, cocking one hand on my hip and tossing my hair with all the sass I could muster.

"But your website says that you accept walk-in appointments on Mondays," Theodore said, running one hand under his mustard yellow suspenders, his eyes narrowed.

"Extenuating circumstances today. Sorry, you have to leave," I said again, edging around the long counter to put some space between Theodore and myself. My hand trailed over a stack of mail on the counter and I almost whimpered in joy when I felt the cool steel of a metal letter opener pass under my hand. Sliding it closer to my body, I waited to see what Theodore would do.

"I really must insist on a reading. Only one question, really. I promise I won't take much of your time." Theodore threw his hands up, smiling easily, everyone's best friend here.

"I don't think so, Theodore, you're up to something. Get out," I said, dropping any pretense of civility.

"Fine, maybe I'll just ask my question right here then," Theodore said, coming to stand on the other side of the counter, his pudgy hands gripping the side so intensely that his pink flesh turned to white. He leaned over until his warm breath wafted over my face.

"Should I leave my wife?"

"Excuse me?" I said, my mouth dropping open as I took several steps back from the counter, keeping the mail opener in my hand, but tucked behind my satchel.

"Should. I. Leave. MY. *WIFE!*" Theodore shouted, spittle flying from his lips onto the counter, rage flashing across his face.

This was the real Theodore, I thought, my hand instinctively tightening around the mail opener.

"I can't answer that for you," I said, honestly.

"Well you certainly had no problem telling her that she should leave me!" Theodore slammed his hands down on the counter, swiping a basket of pens to the floor. My heart hammered in my chest and the only sounds in the room were the pens rolling across the wood floor and Theodore's shaky breath.

"I didn't tell her that," I said softly, searching his eyes.

"You did! Don't you lie to me, Althea. We had a big fight after she saw you the other day. She told me that you said she should leave me. Now she's talking about getting a divorce. How could you?" Theodore's voice cracked on the last word and I swear to God, a sheen of tears sprang into his eyes.

What was going on here?

"Theodore, first of all, I never betray client confidentiality. But, I can most assuredly tell you that I never told her to leave you. In fact, against my better judgment, since I don't like you the slightest bit, I told her she would be happier if she stayed with you, lord knows why," I said, glaring at him across the counter.

"Really?" Theodore swiped his hand across his eyes and straightened, throwing his shoulders back and puffing out his chest.

"Really," I muttered, trying to figure out what his game was. A quick read of his thoughts showed that his rage had vanished and a quiet relief had slipped in.

Well, shoot, color me surprised.

The man really did love his wife.

"Erm, well, I'm sorry about all this then. I guess I'll have to pick up some diamonds or something on the way home. Maybe there's still hope after all," Theodore said, a smile lighting his face as he nodded at me and made his way towards the door.

"Don't mind me! I'll just pick up these pens!" I called, racing to slam the door and lock it after him. Turning, I leaned back against the door for the second time today, forcing myself to calm my breathing. My mind was racing.

If Theodore only hated me because of the reading with his wife – then that only left Cash as an option.

And it wasn't an option I was willing to consider.

Chapter Twenty-Three

MOMENTS LATER, I found myself driving down Main Street towards Luca's Deli, mulling over what had just happened at the shop. I wondered if my reading on Theodore had been totally off and if he was really just a self-important man who was clinging to his beauty queen of a wife. I was more confused now than I had ever been.

Much like any other Monday in Tequila Key, the street had a few moms pushing strollers, and the occasional group of locals chatting on the stoops of various businesses. Mr. Roberts swept the front porch of Fins, and waved casually at me as I drove past. I couldn't help but look at each person and wonder if somehow they were connected to Renaldo's death.

Anyone but Cash would pretty much work for me.

Luca's Deli was tucked at the end of the street in a whitewashed stucco building with little pots of flowers out front that Luca watered religiously. Knowing I would be just missing the lunch rush, I snagged the last spot on the street and kept my head down as I ducked into the deli.

Cool air washed over me, carrying the scents of meatballs and fresh-baked bread. Small tables with cheerful blue tablecloths were clustered together in front of two long glass cases full of mounds of meat, deli-salads, and a jar of the finest pickles you'll taste in all of the Keys.

"Althea!" Luca called to me as he worked from a butcher's block behind the counter. Clad in a screaming-red velour tracksuit and sporting a comb-over to finish off his New Jersey appearance, Luca was all tan skin, white smile, and dancing eyes.

"Hey, Luca," I said, turning to greet Mrs. Evanston at the counter, done up in a resplendent pale pink dress suit and pearls today.

"Althea, I'm so glad to see you. I've just been over the moon ever since you gave me such a good reading," Mrs. Evanston said, pressing her papery lips to my cheek as I bent over to give her a quick hug.

"Althea gave you a reading? Tell you anything interesting?" Luca asked over his shoulder.

"Well, you know she can talk to ghosts, right? So I had her channel my dearly departed cat. You knew Bitsy, right, Luca? She was a show cat – one of the best," Mrs. Evanston said, her blue curls bouncing as she warmed up to her favorite topic.

"Sure I do. Crying shame you lost her," Luca said, winking at me over the counter.

"Well, I certainly do miss her. But now that I know Althea can talk to her, well, I'll just be stopping by every once in a while to check in and make sure my Bitsy's doing okay," Mrs. Evanston said, twinkling up at me.

Oh great.

"I look forward to seeing you, Mrs. Evanston." I smiled down at her.

"Now, you tell your friend Luna that none of us think a sweet girl like her would murder anyone. Why! Just the thought of it makes me so mad. That Dupree better get his head on straight," she said, clucking her tongue in disgust as she took the paper bag Luca offered her.

"Can I get something going for you?" Luca cut in.

"Um, sure, turkey on rye and a chicken on wheat with avocado mayo." Wondering briefly if Trace would be joining us again today as he hadn't bothered to take the time to text me at all, I held up two fingers.

"Make that two turkey on rye. And probably like six pickles," I said with a smile, turning back to Mrs. Evanston.

"Thank you for your concern, Mrs. Evanston. I'll be giving Dupree a piece of my mind after lunch. One way or the other, I'm going to get Luna out as soon as I can."

"You let me know if I can help, dear," she said, patting my arm softly before moving past me to leave.

"That's tough about your friend," Luca said over his shoulder as he slathered mayonnaise on some bread. I bit my tongue just as I was about to make a snide remark about the bets he was taking. Beau was right. Nothing should come between us and one of Luca's decadent sandwiches.

"Well, it's obviously not true, so we need to get her out of there," I said, pulling napkins from the napkin holder and grabbing some of the small packs of mustard that Luca had in a tin basket on the counter.

"Why do you think it's not true?" Luca asked, wrap-

ping our sandwiches in white wax paper and sliding them
into the bag. I waited until he had wrapped our pickles
before replying.

"Because I know she's innocent," I said.

Luca brought the sandwiches over to me and pulled out
a brown paper bag from underneath the counter. Shaking it
open, he smiled kindly at me.

"Knowing isn't enough to prove it in court. You need
evidence."

"Well, I'll get evidence then."

"How? You going to hunt the killer down? Or just
walk around town reading people's minds?" Luca scoffed
and then straightened. "Hey, maybe you could do that?"

"Maybe I will," I said, my nose in the air, reluctant to
admit that that might have been one of the plans that I had
concocted the night before. "And you need to stop running
bets on her being the killer. What's wrong with you,
Luca?" I reached across the counter to smack him on
the arm.

"Hey, hey, hey now…business is business, you know."
Luca shrugged, looking appropriately chastised.

"You've known Luna a long time. You know as well as
I do that she's not the killer," I said, glaring at him.

"Here, I'll throw some cookies in to make up for it,"
Luca said, reaching for his chocolate chunk cookies, but
avoiding answering me. I almost said no.

But nobody says no to Luca's cookies.

"You'd better stop this betting. I mean it, Luca. This
isn't funny," I said, nose in the air.

"Alright, alright," he said, holding his hands up. "It
was just an easy pool to run."

"How could it be easy?" I demanded. "It could be anyone. Literally anyone!"

Luca nodded gravely.

"Long shots make the most money."

"But don't you have to offer odds on certain suspects? People can't just come in and throw money down on anyone, can they?"

Luca blushed a little beneath his tan and I leaned in.

"Luca, who are the top odds?"

"Now, Thea, I can't be telling you that. Books are closed."

"Like hell they are."

The bells over the door jangled and a group of students came in. I huffed out a breath and glared at Luca, knowing this conversation was over. Pointing my finger at him, I gave him my dirtiest look but Luca just shrugged his shoulders with a smile.

People will try to make money off of anything.

Chapter Twenty-Four

MY CELL PHONE rang on the way back to the house and I kept one hand on the wheel as I scrounged in my purse, hitting the button without looking at the screen.

"Hello?"

"It's me."

"Luna!" I shrieked and pulled the car over to the side of the road, startling a woman on a beach cruiser who shot me a dirty look as she passed. I flipped her my middle finger with a smile, not caring what she would think as I focused on my phone.

"Oh my God, Luna, are you okay?" I gushed.

"I'm okay. Just listen. Dupree's in on something. I don't know what. I hear him whispering all the time on the phone. My sense is that he's involved in something and he already knows who the killer is. He's not letting me go anytime soon."

"But doesn't the judge decide that?" I protested.

"I don't know if the judge is involved too," she whispered into the phone and I felt tears swim into my eyes.

"I swear I'm going to fix this for you," I said, clutching the phone against my ear.

"You have to learn the breaking spell. By heart. Tonight. Promise me?" Luna whispered urgently.

"Luna, I can't do a spell without you!" I hissed.

"You can. You just have to mean the words you say. Intent is everything in magic. You've done it with me, you can do it without. Memorize it," Luna said.

"Time's up!" I heard a voice call over her shoulder.

"I'll come to the station today," I promised.

"Don't waste your time. Find the killer," Luna insisted before the call was disconnected. I stared down at my phone, vowing to talk to Miss Elva about the worst curse we could find to ruin Dupree's life.

Hour's up. Where are you?

Two minutes, I texted Beau, pulling back onto the road, my thoughts racing.

I biked to your house. Meet me there.

Reading the text, I whipped a U-turn in the middle of the street, trying not to beat myself up for not accomplishing more. Maybe if I could just calm down, I'd be able to work on getting a clear picture of what direction we needed to go in.

Hank's ears poked over the windowsill when I pulled up. Grabbing the bag of food, I made my way to the porch, bending automatically to accept Hank's licks on my face before straightening.

"Oh. Hey," I said, coming up short as my eyes fell on Cash sitting at my breakfast bar. He looked way too good cozied up to the counter and I entertained a brief fantasy of serving him coffee after a long night of...

"Althea," Beau snapped and I shook my head.

"Yes? Did I miss something?"

"I asked you if you were okay. You look like you've been crying," Beau said, shaking his head at me as he came forward to take the bag of food from my hands.

"I don't even know where to start," I said stiffly, shifting my eyes to Cash, unsure of how much I could say in front of him.

"Start with why you are crying," Beau decided and I went to stand with him on the other side of the counter, turning to pull plates out of one of my cabinets.

"Luna called." I shrugged.

"She did! How is she? Can we see her?"

"She said not to waste our time. That we needed to stay focused," I said instead, again looking over my shoulder at Cash, trying not to act suspicious.

"I get the feeling I'm not wanted here," Cash said, pushing back from the counter and standing up.

"It's not that…" I protested, but then stopped, unsure of what to say. That I thought he could be the killer? Not caring if it was rude, I dipped into his mind.

And all I got was genuine concern for my welfare.

What if he was smart enough to know that I was a psychic and decided to just think good thoughts while around me? My eyebrows shot up at the thought and Cash tilted his head at me in question.

"It's just…look, there's a lot going on right now. Luna's our best friend. If you wouldn't mind giving us a little space?" I asked gently, surprised to see a small flash of hurt on Cash's face before he nodded.

"Of course, I understand. Let me know if I can help with anything," Cash said, turning to go.

"Actually, you can," Beau said and I whipped my head around to glare at him.

"What? I have questions," Beau said simply, widening his eyes innocently at me.

"So you make me look like the mean one?" I asked, putting my hands on my waist and glaring at Beau.

"It's not making you look mean. It's just a confusing time. He may have answers," Beau said, turning to smile at Cash.

"I'm happy to help," Cash said again, his gaze meeting mine.

"Okay, well, I have an extra sandwich," I said, praying that Trace didn't come by and want to eat.

"I'm good, I ate before I stopped by," Cash said, clearly knowing whom the third sandwich was for.

I glared at Beau again before shoving Trace's sandwich into the fridge.

"Something to drink then?"

"Got a beer?"

"This early?" I asked and then stopped. Shoot, we could all use a drink for what we were dealing with. "Never mind, we'll all have beers," I mumbled, and grabbed a bucket to fill with ice.

"We'll be on the patio?" Beau asked.

I shooed him away and filled the bucket, plopping some Coronas amongst the ice, then sliced up some limes before I joined them on the patio. Hank raced in circles around the yard, ecstatic that Mom was home on a Monday.

"He's got a lot of energy," Cash commented.

"Boston terriers are spunky," I agreed, before choosing a seat opposite Cash instead of sitting next to him on the couch. So what if I was giving him mixed signals? I had a murder to solve.

"So, Beau. Questions?" Cash said, taking a long pull of his beer.

"Yes, Beau. Questions?" I said, turning to smile brightly at Beau.

"You worked with Renaldo before, yes?" Beau asked and I finally realized where he was going with his questions.

"I wouldn't say worked with. We've been on the other side of the table in a few negotiations, though," Cash said.

"What was he like?" I blurted out.

"As a businessman? He seemed fair. Steady to do business with. I never got the sense that he was trying to be underhanded or anything."

"Why was he in town?" I countered.

"He was looking at a few different properties for development," Cash said.

"Can you be more specific?" Beau asked.

"I wish. He represented a competing investment group. Though I was kind of surprised to see him here. Last I had heard, he was planning to retire," Cash mused.

"Well, that's weird, isn't it?" I said, turning to Beau.

"So as a consultant...he did what exactly?"

"The dealings that I had with him in Miami, he'd represent a group of investors. For example, we worked on a nightclub together. That kind of thing," Cash said.

"And nothing ever popped as weird to you?"

"No, not that I can think of. Granted, I didn't like how the guy dressed, but that isn't enough to murder him for," Cash said easily and I stiffened, wondering if he thought we suspected him.

"No, of course not. Though I agree on the clothes," Beau said smoothly and I nodded.

"Me three. Too slick," I agreed and Cash flashed me a smile that caused my insides to tingle and had me reaching for my beer.

"So who is S&L Investments?" I asked, wiping my mouth with my napkin, watching Cash carefully.

"S&L? Never heard of them," he said. A quick scan told me that he wasn't lying.

"Some online sleuthing seemed to suggest that Renaldo was working with them," Beau explained.

"Ah, so that was his investment group. He'd never mentioned who he was with this time. I can ask around," Cash said and I interrupted.

"Don't. What if you asking questions where questions don't need to be asked gets you hurt?" I asked anxiously, biting my lower lip again.

A slow smile slid across Cash's face and I found myself blushing.

"Worried about me, sweetheart?"

"I'm just saying…" I protested, grabbing my sandwich and stuffing it in my mouth so as to avoid saying anything to embarrass myself.

"Don't you think asking all these questions might be putting you and Beau in danger?" Cash countered and I almost choked on my food.

Beau whacked me on the back, causing me to lurch

forward. Glaring at him, I took a demure sip of my beer and smoothed my napkin onto my lap again.

Cash looked between the two of us and sighed, shaking his head as he rose.

"I'll look into it. Promise me you two won't do anything stupid."

"Of course not," Beau gushed and Cash shook his head again.

"Althea. You and I have things to discuss when this is all over," Cash said, pinning me with his stare. I swallowed, and nodded.

"Aye, aye, Captain," I said and then blushed, wanting to bury my face in my hands. What made me say these weird things?

"Please don't make any 'captaining her ship' jokes," Beau begged as he led Cash to the front door and I groaned.

A lick at my hand had me looking down into Hank's eager smushface, his whole body wriggling as he looked up at me.

"You're my one true love, Hank," I said, reaching down to scratch him.

"Oh God, soon you'll be collecting cats," Beau sang out from the other room and I shot him the middle finger, knowing he couldn't see it.

It made me feel better... for a second, anyways.

Chapter Twenty-Five

AFTER A FEW UNSUCCESSFUL hours of searching the Internet, I found myself pacing my private beach with Hank when I heard a voice calling to me.

I stiffened, unsure of my response.

Trace.

When had my life become so complicated? I turned, smiling at him as he walked down to the beach from my yard. A hint of blond scruff at his jaw added to his overall surfer appearance, and his smile seemed to make things better. Even if just for a moment.

"Hey, I wondered when we would hear from you," I said, wishing I could see his eyes behind his sunglasses.

"I was doing some investigating on my own. Plus, I needed some time to chill out," Trace admitted.

I looked down at the sand where I was tracing a line with my big toe.

"I get that," I said finally.

"I don't want things to get weird between us. Let's just…I don't know. Let's talk after we get Luna out, okay?"

Trace said and I felt relief wash over me even though a flash of sadness came with that relief. It was too hard for me to know my own mind on this stuff right now and I knew what Trace suggested was the mature thing to do.

"Yes, after all this. We can talk. I heard from Luna," I said, changing the subject and pushing away the thought of the two serious conversations that I'd be having with the men in my life.

"What did she say?"

"She swears Dupree is in on this. Oh, shoot!" I said, remembering her insistence on my learning the breaking spell.

"What?"

"She wants me to learn a breaking spell. By heart. Tonight. I wonder what that means for me?" I realized suddenly that her insistence should have served as a warning.

"Um, duh, you need to watch your back. Luna knows what's what," Trace said, matching my pace as we walked back to my house.

"Well, I haven't really been going anywhere. I was considering sitting down and trying to get another vision. Or even walking around the town to read some people's thoughts." I shrugged, feeling a little foolish. Some private investigator I was.

"You should probably try to stay out of the town," Trace suggested, stopping as we reached my house. "Though I do think we should dive in the morning."

"You do?" I said, turning to him questioningly. How could he think that going underwater was going to help anything?

"Yeah, I do. Notice how Dupree never had anyone go back to check out the ocean floor? I can't help but wonder if anything else was thrown overboard along with Renaldo."

"That's...an excellent point. I never thought about it." A shiver raced through me as I thought about going back to the site where we had found his body.

"It'll be fine. You can't let this ruin your love for diving," Trace said, reaching out to run his hand down my arm.

"What are y'all talking about?" Beau called.

"I think we should go diving in the morning. Check out if anything else was tossed overboard along with Renaldo," Trace said, moving to plop down on my patio couch. I couldn't help but think that Cash had just filled that spot hours ago. Two men, two wildly different looks and personalities.

I was doomed.

"That's not a half-bad idea," Beau said, coming onto the patio and handing Trace a plate with a sandwich.

"Okay, I'll do it. But first I need to memorize this spell," I mumbled, going into the kitchen to where my purse stood. Pulling out the white suede book, I ran my hands over it, feeling the powerful hum that resonated from the book and knowing that Luna had charmed the pages. I wondered if something would happen to me if I tried to open it.

"No way," I said out loud, but remembering Luna's instructions about intent, I placed my hand on the book and sent my intention to it that I wished to cause no harm. I pulled at the leather cord, and the flap slid open seamlessly, the soft suede like butter in my hands as I gently opened the book.

"Breaking spell," I murmured as I paged through, admiring the dignified handwriting with just the hint of loopiness in the L's. Everything about Luna was classy, including her spell book, I mused.

"Ah, here we go," I said, pausing as I read the instructions of the breaking spell.

To use in breaking bonds, both physical and emotional, that hold you back from your purpose.

"Well that certainly casts a wide net," I said again as I scanned the spell. I wondered if she wanted me to break a relationship bond…maybe with Cash? Nibbling at my bottom lip, I scanned the words.

Undo this bond
   At once set me free
   As I must respond
   For my light is in need
   As I will, so mote it be.

Seemed pretty straightforward, I thought as I flipped to the next page to see if there was anything weird I had to do like cut a lock of hair or draw a circle. The next page held a new spell, so from my estimation, all I needed to do was intend for the spell to work.

"How's it going?" Trace asked as he came into the room.

"Fine, I should be able to remember this. I just wish I knew what I was preparing for."

"Beau is going to stay with you tonight. I need to go home and check our tanks very carefully, gas up the boat, look for any foul play-type stuff. Just in case." Trace shrugged his shoulders nonchalantly and I straightened in my seat.

"Shouldn't someone come with you?" I worried.

"Chill, Althea. I've got a gun."

"You do?" I said, my mouth dropping open. Easygoing Trace did not strike me as someone who carried a gun.

"I've lived on my own and moved around a lot. I'm an excellent shot." Trace smiled briefly before dropping a chaste kiss on my cheek.

"See you tomorrow, then. Be safe," I said, pressing my hand to his cheek for a moment.

"Thanks, Mom," Trace called over his shoulder, causing me to chuckle, as well as putting me right back in the friend category.

"Okay then. This will all work out." I blew out a breath as I focused on the words in front of me, praying I would never have to use them.

We would just have to see what tomorrow brings, I thought.

Chapter Twenty-Six

"ARE YOU SURE you don't want me to drive you to the wharf?" Beau asked, worry creeping into his voice as he paced in front of me, Hank in his arms.

"It's fine," I said, packing my dive bag.

In all reality, I wanted to stop at Miss Elva's without Beau scoffing at me. We had differing opinions of the voodoo priestess and I didn't want to hear it.

"You will text me when you arrive?"

"I promise to text you the minute that I step on the boat and am in Trace's capable hands," I said.

"Fine, I'll stay here with Hank for a bit and wait to hear from Cash. He said he had uncovered some stuff that could be of use to us."

"Lord, I hope so. I'm really nervous about the hearing tomorrow," I said, pulling the straps of the dive bag over my shoulder. Today I wore a more modest bikini, along with a tank top and shorts with pockets for me to slip my phone into instead of a beach cover-up and my phone in my bag. See? I was being careful.

"I don't trust Dupree. And I still don't trust Theodore," Beau said. I had told him about my run-in with Theodore at the shop. We'd come to two conclusions. Either Theodore was madly in love with his wife and furious at me – or he was trying to throw me off the scent.

"I don't trust either of them. But they both have to know I won't sit around and do nothing while my best friend is locked up. I promise to stay alert."

"I'll text you after Cash comes by."

I stopped at the door and turned.

"He's coming by?"

"Does that bother you?"

"Well, what if…" I shrugged, not wanting to say it.

"Althea Rose, you can't think that man is the killer."

"I don't. But…I can't dismiss it. I just need to know for sure," I admitted.

"Do you get any reading from him that says differently?"

"No." I shrugged helplessly, still nervous to leave.

"Fine, I'll meet him in town," Beau sighed.

"Thank you," I breathed, leaning over to kiss his cheek.

"Your mommy's crazy," I heard Beau telling Hank as I closed the door.

Maybe I was, at that.

The light was still soft this early in the morning, and a slight breeze tickled my face as I biked to Miss Elva's. An iguana skittered out of my path, but aside from that, my ride was peaceful. Though this town had its share of issues, I loved Tequila Key in the mornings, when the soft light didn't reveal the wear and tear on the buildings, and the only sounds were the birds and the ocean.

Knowing Miss Elva would be up – I swear that woman never sleeps – I pulled my bike to a stop in front of her house and leaned it against the chain-link fence. Debating whether I should knock or go around to the back, I jumped when her voice called to me from a dark corner of the porch.

"Shoot, Miss Elva, you're going to give me a heart attack if you keep lurking in dark corners," I said as I walked up the steps to the porch.

"Maybe you shouldn't be sneaking up on someone's property so you wouldn't be getting so startled," Miss Elva said, rocking slowly in her weathered wood rocking chair. Today her hair was wrapped in a cloth the color of raspberries with sprinkles of turquoise throughout. Wearing a matching caftan and cradling a shotgun on her lap, Miss Elva was nothing short of terrifying.

"Um, what's with the shotgun?" I asked nervously. Miss Elva nodded at me to sit and so I took a thin wooden straight-backed chair next to her. The visitor chair said everything you needed to know about Miss Elva.

You're welcome here, but don't overstay your welcome.

I shifted in the uncomfortable chair and waited for Miss Elva to speak. She was a woman worth listening to, in my opinion.

"Evil's in the air," Miss Elva said simply.

"Don't I know it," I muttered.

"You come here for protection." It was a statement, not a question.

"Actually, no. I came here because I want to know…" I

dropped my voice and looked around to make sure the other porches nearby were clear. "I want to know how to curse Chief Dupree."

"Nasty man," Miss Elva agreed.

"He's doing something bad. And Luna's taking the fall."

"I heard. Poor girl. You'll get her out. I already worked up a few things for you," Miss Elva said, rocking backwards and then forward again to launch herself into a standing position. I winced, keeping my eyes on the shotgun.

"You knew I was coming?"

"Do you really need to ask that?" Miss Elva raised an eyebrow at me, and with her gun, she held the screen door open to her house.

"Right," I said, blowing out a breath as I gingerly stepped past the shotgun and into Miss Elva's house.

I'd been inside once before but not for long enough to appease my curiosity. It certainly put my eccentric little shop to shame, I thought as I scanned the thousands of knick-knacks, bottles, feathers, and various other containers that lined the walls of her house. Yes, *thousands*.

It was like an homage to the voodoo arts without there being any discernable organization or theme. A Pottery Barn catalog was topped with a monkey skull on the living room table, and peacock feathers stuck out of what I presumed was an urn.

"Come, come," Miss Elva said, ushering me through a narrow hallway to a surprisingly spotless kitchen. A butcher-block table stood in the middle along with four stools. On the table stood several blue glass bottles, a few leather bags, and a mortar and pestle.

"Sit." Miss Elva pointed and propped the gun in the corner as I slid myself onto the chair and looked down at the items in front of me.

"This is curse stuff?"

"This is your protection. A curse, or in this case probably a hex would be better, is a little more involved. A hex takes more effort and ritual, which also gives you some time to cool off, so you don't go around hexing people every time you get your mad on. And, sometimes, that time allows the universe to right itself without any intervention from you at all," Miss Elva said as she pulled the mortar towards her and began to dash various ingredients from the bottles into the bowl. She looked down her nose at me to make sure that I understood.

"Sometimes it's best to let the bad people bury themselves?" I asked.

"Yes. But I'll work on something. I will make the choice on how to handle this. Not you. Understood?"

"Yes, ma'am," I said, feeling my shoulders slump like I was being scolded.

"Now, this?" Miss Elva held up the bowl and I nodded. "This is your protection. Put the bag in your pocket. Do not drop it. Throw it when you need it."

"How will I know when I need it?" I asked, my eyes widening.

"You'll know."

"What does it do?" I asked in awe as she poured the freshly-ground ingredients into a small pouch.

"Shush, girl." Miss Elva shot me a glare and then

focused back on the pouch. I strained to hear what she was mumbling but I couldn't understand her words.

"There. All done." Miss Elva nodded and then handed me the small pouch. I took it gingerly, desperately wishing that I knew what it was for.

"Um, thanks. Do I owe you anything?"

"Hmpf." Miss Elva looked highly offended. "Put it in your shorts. Right now, while I am watching you," she ordered, clearly not having forgiven me for forgetting the gris-gris.

I slipped from the stool and slid the pouch into the back pocket of my shorts, on the other side from my phone.

"This good? Will I explode if I sit on it?"

Miss Elva began to heave and I realized that she was laughing – it was like watching an earthquake shake a mountain.

"It does exactly what you need it to, when you need it to."

And that, my friends, was that.

Chapter Twenty-Seven

I WOULD BE LYING if I said I didn't have some trepidation about going diving after stopping at Miss Elva's and being handed a protection something-or-another that was now shoved in my pocket. I'd never been accused of being stupid before, and with two not-so-subtle warnings under my belt now, I was on high alert.

Stopping at the top of the docks, I locked my bike and scanned the boats, looking for any unusual activity. The usual fleet of fishermen stocked their boats, and Trace's boat rocked gently in the water at the end of the pier. I didn't see him moving around on board, but I assumed he was here as he always made it to the docks before I did.

Starting down the main dock, I nodded at the regulars in their boats, finding it increasingly difficult to step closer to Trace's boat. My mental radar was sending alarms that something was seriously wrong – I just didn't know what. With every step closer to the boat, my anxiety increased. Was the boat going to explode? I wondered if I shouldn't go any closer. I reached the end of the dock and hesitated about stepping onto the small pier that would allow me to board the boat. My gaze traced the boat, looking for anything off.

When I saw a hand sticking out from under the bench, palm facing up, I almost screamed.

"No, no, no, no," I gasped, rushing to jump onto the boat, not looking around me, only knowing that I had to help Trace.

"Althea. So nice of you to join us."

The voice made my heart drop into my stomach. I didn't want to turn – didn't want it to be the person I knew the voice belonged to.

I'd been listening to it for almost all of my life.

Chapter Twenty-Eight

"LUCA," I GASPED, turning to stare at my favorite deli-shop owner, my mind clouded with the pain of knowing that someone who was a fixture in this town – in my life – was actually a killer.

"Hands up, Althea," Luca ordered, his face grim, the gun he was holding in his hand as steady as could be. I held my hands up, dropping my eyes to where Trace lay unconscious under the bench.

"Trace," I moaned, my heart jumping into my throat. A bead of sweat trickled down my back.

"He's fine. Take your bag off – slowly," Luca ordered, his eyes holding mine, his meaning clear.

"Okay," I said, praying that I didn't drop the bag or do something klutzy to set him off. I slipped the straps of the bag from my shoulders quickly, letting the bag fall with a thud behind me. Why wasn't anyone helping us? Couldn't they see what was happening?

"Turn around," Luca said. "If you say anything – lover boy gets a bullet in the brain."

I choked back a sob and nodded, turning my back to Luca, saying a silent prayer that this wouldn't be the end for Trace and I.

The touch of his hands at my wrists made me jump. I closed my eyes as he wrenched my arms back, and I heard the zip of a zip-tie as he bound my wrists together.

I gasped as Luca kicked the backs of my knees, forcing me to the bottom of the boat.

"If you move, one inch, he's done," Luca ordered and moved to the top of the boat to unloop the line from the deck. I scanned Trace, praying that he would come to soon, noticing that his hands weren't tied.

Oh, this could get ugly.

Unsure if talking would set Luca off, I bit my lip and watched as he stood at the wheel – wearing a blue tracksuit today – with aviators concealing his eyes. I couldn't imagine what had brought him to do this. The man ran a successful business. He had a girlfriend he was going to travel Europe with.

Or did he?

Wondering how much of Luca's life was a lie, I pressed back against the leg of the bench, dully watching the docks grow smaller, wondering just how I was going to get myself out of this. Wouldn't someone at the docks wonder why Luca was driving Trace's boat? I wondered if the large canopy had concealed Luca's activities from the fishermen.

Or maybe they just didn't care.

I squeezed my eyes shut and waited until the boat had moved further down the canal that would lead us out to the ocean. Figuring I could talk now that we were further from the docks, I looked up at Luca.

"Where are we going?"

"To Baker's Island."

I groaned and all but bit through my bottom lip. Baker's Island was a private island off the coast. Think million-dollar yachts and a private airstrip. I had no idea who owned it and I suspected that I wasn't going to like finding out.

Luca set the GPS and then stepped away from the wheel, bending over Trace, his gun ready in case Trace suddenly moved. I prayed he wouldn't do anything stupid, like trying to lunge at Luca and get the gun.

Luca reached out and flipped Trace around, quickly zip-tying his hands together as well. I cringed as I watched Trace's face being pressed into the rubber dive mats on the floor, a bruise blossoming across his forehead.

"That's just in case lover boy here decides to get any ideas when he wakes up," Luca said cheerfully.

"He's not my lover," I said softly, watching Luca.

"He's not? Hmm, I read that situation wrong."

"Why are you doing this?" I asked, making Luca pause as he checked the GPS again and adjusted the wheel a bit to correct our course. Turning, Luca sat on the bench behind the wheel and crossed his arms over his chest, leaning back thoughtfully. He looked like a grandfather about to tell his grandkids a story.

"Well, I'm not actually too pleased about the two of you but I realized I had to nip this loose end in the bud once you came into the shop yesterday. It was something Mrs. Evanston said about being able to read people's minds that had me thinking it might be best to take care of this situation," Luca sighed, and shook his head at me. "You had to go and try to solve this, didn't you?"

"She's my best friend," I protested.

"Yes, that's unfortunate. I've always liked you two. Tip well and don't leave a mess in my shop. Damn shame," he sighed again, shaking his head like there was nothing he could do about it.

"So change it," I begged.

"Sorry, no can do. Luna set herself up perfectly for being the fall guy – or girl, in this instance – by having a little rendezvous with Renaldo the night we decided to off him. Ah love, it'll kill you." Luca laughed at his joke, bending over to slap his leg like I've seen him do so many times before. Except this time his laugh sounded sinister to me.

"What did Renaldo know that you didn't want him to know?" I asked, trying to keep him talking. Luca shifted slightly to grab the wheel and keep us on course before turning back to me.

"I suppose I can tell you now, as you won't be getting out of this," Luca mused, running his fingers over his chin thoughtfully.

A wash of ice hit my stomach and I felt my body begin to tremble, adrenalin starting to surge as I began to move into panic mode.

"Renaldo was going to snitch," Luca said simply.

"Snitch on what exactly?"

"Ah, well, you know, Tequila Key is actually fairly well positioned for a stop on the way up from the islands. It's easy to drop things off and feed them up to Miami from here," Luca began and I just started shaking my head at him.

"What?"

"Drugs. You're doing this because of drugs."

"Well, Missy, it's not like I'm on the corner with a dime bag of weed. This is millions of dollars in drugs."

"How did you get involved in this?" I wondered if Luca had been a drug dealer his whole life. Suddenly his tracksuit and gold chain weren't so charming anymore.

"Ah, well, I was approached by an investment group."

"S&L?"

"That's the one! See? I told you you shouldn't have gone around asking questions." Luca shook his head sadly at me.

"Anywho, they approached me and offered me a cold two million for the deli, so long as I disappeared but they could still keep operating it as a deli. They'd run the drugs, and the drug money, through the business. Keep it all very mom and pop – local, you know," Luca said.

"And you said yes?"

"That's two million dollars, baby! You tell me if you could say no to that?"

I looked at Luca, my eyes wide.

"Yeah, I could. I really could. Studies show you only need about $70,000 a year to be truly happy, you know," I said, realizing that I was almost babbling.

"You don't say? Huh, never read that one. Anyways, Renaldo was representing S&L in finding them a place."

"So Renaldo was in on it?"

Luca shook his head.

"Nope. Poor guy found out after they had solicited his

help in negotiating a commercial license with me. They hacked his computer and found out he planned to snitch. So…" Luca threw up his hands. "Sleeping with da fishes!"

He grinned like he'd been waiting his entire life to say that phrase.

"So you never were really going off to Europe with a girlfriend then?" I asked.

"Of course I'm going to Europe with a girlfriend. Or several of them. With all this money? See ya later, Tequila Key." Luca laughed and then straightened as Baker's Island began to come into view. "Ah, we're close now. I'm just the delivery boy. I doubt you'll get out of this one alive, but hey, at least it won't be on my hands." Luca hummed softly to himself as I looked at him in disbelief. Where was the happy-go-lucky man I had known almost my whole life?

Though, admittedly, he still seemed pretty happy right now – which really creeped me out.

"So that's it? I die, Trace dies, Luna gets life in prison and you go on your merry way?" My voice cracked.

Luca tossed a glance my way. "Sorry, sugar. I'll be long gone by tonight. I hope that I don't have to be the one to kill you. That'd be a crying shame."

This man was a freaking lunatic.

All I could do was hang my head and wait while he slowed the motor and began to putter into the bay of Baker's Island.

Our fate awaited us at the dock.

Chapter Twenty-Nine

I CLOSED MY EYES, not wanting to see who the voices belonged to that Luca was cheerfully chatting with as he tied up Trace's boat. Then a moan from across the floor caused my eyes to pop right back open.

"Trace," I hissed, holding my breath as his eyes began to open.

His eyelashes fluttered and I could see the haze in his eyes clear as he looked around, remembering where he was. His arms jerked as he pulled against his bonds and realized that his hands were bound.

"Luca," Trace said urgently.

"I know," I said, grimacing at him.

"Ah, I see sleeping beauty has awoken." Luca's voice floated down to us from the front of the boat and I turned, gasping as I saw the man next to him.

"Dupree," I spit out.

"That's Chief Dupree to you, Ms. Rose," Chief Dupree drawled as he hopped onto the boat. "You seem to have trouble remembering that."

"How could you? You're a police officer!" I exclaimed, surging up to my feet, rage flitting through me.

Rage because I knew that if Dupree were involved, then somehow they would pin it all on Luna. And my best friend would look like a murderer while we joined Renaldo in a watery grave.

"They were going to bring a lot of money into this town. And a lot of payoff money into my pocket." Dupree smiled lazily at me. "You think I want to spend the rest of my life on a state salary while writing up loitering tickets to teens skateboarding at the park? I don't think so."

"You can't do this!" I cried.

"He can, Thea. Just sit down. There's nothing we can do," Trace said, his voice resigned.

"How can you say that?" I hissed at him, feeling betrayed by his attitude.

Trace just shrugged but wouldn't meet my eyes.

So I sat on the bench and waited to see what they would do next, so furious that I could barely think straight. Dupree and Luca both left the boat and walked down the dock, meeting someone who was strapped with more ammo than Rambo before turning to point at us.

"Pssst," Trace whispered and I slid a glance across at him.

"Your phone is in your back pocket, I saw it sticking out a bit. Can you pull it out and give it to me?"

My phone. I'd completely forgotten that I had it tucked in my back pocket. With my hands behind my back, it was easy for me to wrap my fingers around.

"Hold up, they're here. Let's just wait until they put us

wherever they are going to put us, and then I can reach in your pocket and call."

I nodded, slipping my phone into my waistband at my back, where my loose tank top would cover it. I prayed they wouldn't frisk us.

"Alright, you two degenerates, let's go," Dupree called, chuckling at his little joke. Yeah, we all knew who the degenerates here were.

It took everything in my power not to knee him between the legs when he walked past me to grab my arm, but I knew it would only worsen our predicament.

Well, that and the man pointing a high-caliber silencer at my head. Rambo was on the dock, his gun trained on us, his gaze unwavering. I had a very childish urge to push him into the water as I stepped from the boat and walked past him. A giggle bubbled up in my throat and I did my best to suppress it. A small snort escaped anyway.

"Are you laughing?" Dupree asked incredulously.

"Sorry," I giggled, "nervous laughter. Like in church." I snorted again and then forced myself to breath.

"You shouldn't be laughing in church. What's wrong with you?" Dupree asked.

"You've got to be kidding me." I rolled my eyes.

"Probably because you're into all that occult crap. Tequila Key will be better off not having you two Satan worshipers around," Dupree declared, already fabricating his story.

"Oh, that's rich. Just freaking unbelievable," I muttered, my nervous laughter gone as cold reality settled onto my shoulders. At the end of the dock, Dupree forced us to walk across a small sand beach. I could barely look up as I was tripping in my flip-flops in the sand, but from what I could see, we were being led towards an almost all-glass compound of sorts.

"Nice place, huh?" Dupree asked.

"Yup, just fabulous. I'm sure with all the money you're making from killing us, you'll be able to set yourself up real nice," I said and cringed, waiting for a backhand to come.

"Watch your mouth. Keep it up and I just might be the one to kill you after all." Dupree smirked. I wanted to slam my elbow back into his paunchy gut.

"To the right here," Dupree called back to Luca, who was presumably leading Trace.

Dupree veered off from the path to the glass house and instead followed a little dirt trail towards a concrete building. Two doors on the front were padlocked closed and I had a pretty good idea where we were ending up.

"We'll keep you here until we can motor out on the water tonight," Dupree explained, nodding his thanks to Rambo when he unlocked the padlock and opened the door. As the light sliced into the room, I realized it must be some sort of storage for jet skis or kayaks, as there were a few platforms in the back.

No windows. And only one way out.

"Oof." I glared at Dupree as he pushed me forward, forcing me to duck just a little to get into the concrete shed.

"Sit," Dupree said.

I turned to sit and then he stopped me.

"Oh, I almost forgot. Gosh, I haven't had to do this in a

while in our sleepy little town." Dupree grimaced and then began to pat me down.

I held my breath, praying that he wouldn't find my phone, unable to look at Trace.

"Ah-ha!" Dupree crowed gleefully, his hand having crossed my phone. "Sorry, dear. You don't get one phone call from this prison."

With that, they turned, slamming the door behind them.

The click of the padlock had to be the worst sound that I've ever heard in my life.

Chapter Thirty

"YOU'VE GOT TO be kidding me," I shrieked.

"Calm down, Althea," Trace ordered.

"Calm down? A week ago the biggest worry I had was what sandwich to order from Luca's. And now my best friend's in jail and we're about to die." I began to heave as panic ricocheted through me, and I knew I was moments away from a full-blown panic attack.

"Hey, shhh, it's okay," Trace said. I could see him moving in the dim light that peeked from the line beneath the door. He moved across the floor until his back was on the same wall as mine and bumped shoulders with me.

"How can you say that?" I whispered, turning to look at him even though I could barely see his face.

"Because you're a fighter. It's one of the qualities I love about you."

And there it was.

The big L word.

I let it hang between us for a moment, testing to see if I

felt the same way about him. I loved Trace. But was I *in* love with him?

"Thea, I...I," Trace began and I cut him off.

"Trace. Don't," I whispered, shaking my head back and forth frantically.

"Don't? Why?" Trace said and I could hear the hurt creeping into his voice.

"I don't want you to tell me that under duress. It can't be because you think you're going to die. It has to be like randomly, some Tuesday, when we're getting back from a dive or something. Not like this."

"Thea, that's not fair."

"No, it is fair," I insisted. "People say all sorts of stuff when they think they are about to die. Listen, I love you and you're one of my best friends. And I know you love me too. But the *in* love part? Let's just leave that for another day."

I heard a shaky sigh from him and I prayed that I hadn't hurt his feelings too badly.

"See? Now you're talking like we'll live. At least you aren't panicking anymore," Trace said and I could hear the smile in his voice.

"So help me...if that was just a ruse to get my mind off of losing it," I threatened, but found that he was right. My panic had lessened a bit and it seemed like I would be able to think more clearly.

"I'd never joke about something like that," Trace said, bumping my shoulder again and this time I felt my heart clench a bit in my chest.

"What do we do now?"

"We wait. And think. We have until tonight, right? Isn't that what they said?"

"Yes, I believe so."

I shivered at the thought of going out on the boat with them, motoring quietly out into dark waters, having a chain wrapped slowly around my ankles.

"Good, that gives us at least the day. Time to be MacGyver," Trace said and stood, slowly making his way around the small room.

"What are you doing?"

"Looking for a tool to break these bonds on our wrists."

Bonds.

If my hands were free I would have slapped myself in the forehead.

"Trace!" I said, ecstatic.

"What?"

"The breaking spell! I thought it was maybe something to do with relationships. But it's meant to break physical bonds too!"

Trace hurried back to me and kneeled in front of where I sat. I could just see a gleam in his eyes in the dull light.

"Please tell me you memorized it."

"I did!"

"I'm not sure how to modify it to do your bonds though," I said, wondering if the spell would work on both of us.

"That's okay. If you get yours off, we can figure out a way to cut mine open," Trace said, excitement lacing his voice.

"Okay, hold on. Let me get centered," I said.

Closing my eyes, I took a deep breath and brought myself back to my kitchen counter. I pictured Hank wiggling with joy under my stool, Beau out on the patio and the spell book in front of me on the counter. In my mind, I read through the words again and, satisfied that I remembered the spell, I began.

Focusing on the zip-tie around my wrists, I spoke with strong intention, my voice ringing clear through the shed.

Undo this bond
    At once set me free
    As I must respond
    For my light is in need
    As I will, so mote it be.

I tugged at my hands – and just like that, they were free.

"It worked!" I hissed, reaching forward to grab Trace in a hug. He leaned awkwardly into me, his hands still tied behind his back. He chuckled softly into my neck and my heart sang. There had to be a way out of this for us.

"Luna would be very proud," Trace said softly.

"I'm going to try modifying the spell for you."

Trace sat quietly, his eyes searching mine as I took a deep breath and focused, thinking about what I would say.

Undo this bond
    At once set Trace free
    As he must respond

For his light is in need
As I will, so mote it be.

"Holy shit," Trace whispered as his hands broke free from behind his back. He caught me in a bear hug and we tumbled to the floor, so giddy at being released that we didn't care.

"It worked! I can do magic!" I laughed, even though my arms stung with pain from hours of being tied behind my back.

"You can work your magic on me anytime," Trace leered, and I found myself laughing at him, knowing that we could flirt and joke and it would be okay. One way or the other. It just had to be.

Chapter Thirty-One

A WHILE LATER – it could have been three hours or twenty minutes for all I knew – Trace sat down with a frustrated sigh.

"There is literally nothing in here that I can use to take the hinges off of these doors." Defeated, he banged his hand against his head.

"Hey, you tried," I said, hating that we had gotten such a rush from freeing our hands but were now feeling like we were stuck again.

"Do you think anyone will come looking for us?" Trace asked wearily.

Yes.

Oh, so absolutely yes.

"Trace! Beau will be looking for us. He told me to text him when I got to the docks and I never did. Yesterday when I went a minute past when I was supposed to text, he texted me right away!"

"But they have your phone. Don't you think they'll text him back?"

"Not unless they figure out my code, silly," I sang, feeling happy and knowing that help was on the way.

"There's just one problem with that."

"What?"

"How will he know where we went?"

"Shit," I said, coming quickly down from that little high I was on.

"Can you like...read his mind or something? Send him a message?"

Trace was making a circular motion by his head with his finger that would normally imply that someone was crazy, but I caught his drift.

"Hmm, that's an excellent question. I suppose I've never really tried to do any long-distance type of telepathy," I mused.

"No time like the present, dear," Trace said drolly.

"Yes, I suppose now would be as good a time as any," I said primly and then waved at him to shush up.

Closing my eyes again, I drew a deep breath in through my nose, centering myself, and dropped my mental shields. To orientate myself, I began to scan the area closest to me. I caught a wisp of Trace's mental signature but moved on quickly before I dipped too far into whatever he had going on in there. Lord knows it would distract me. Moving on, I expanded my reach to outside of the concrete bunker we were in.

"I'm picking up some mental signatures a ways from here. Probably like down by the beach or dock. Maybe on a patio. At least three of them. It seems like it's Rambo, Dupree, and Luca."

"Anyone in the house?"

"Hmm," I said, casting a wider net and picking up four more mental signatures inside the house.

"Four inside."

"Seven total, three standing guard."

"Pretty much."

"Can you go off the island?"

"Let me try."

Blowing out a breath, I opened my mind, allowing my astral self to travel past the island. And gasped when what sounded like a voice on a loudspeaker was shouting my name.

"Althea! So help me God, I pray you can hear me. We are coming."

"Did you hear that?" I gasped, convinced that the voice had been outside on a bullhorn it had come through so loudly.

"Nothing?" Trace asked in confusion.

"It's Cash. It's Cash! He must be like screaming to me in his head or something. They're coming!"

"That guy," Trace said, derision in his voice.

"Shut up so I can listen," I said.

"We are on a boat close to the island. I wish I knew where they were keeping you," Cash was thinking.

"Shit," I whispered.

"What?" Trace hissed.

"He's on a boat but they don't know where they are keeping us."

"Well, send him a mental image of where we are? Duh," Trace said, shaking his head at me.

"Oh, you think this is so easy? It's not like I can just

shoot him a text message with a picture of where we are," I said, glaring at Trace.

"Would you just? Close your eyes and focus, woman," Trace hissed again.

"Fine, but I'm going to remember your attitude," I said on a sniff and closed my eyes again to focus on Cash's mental signature. Finding it again, I couldn't help but feel his wash of concern for us and in that instant, I knew what a truly good man he was.

"Cash, we are in the concrete bunker to the right of the house," I said urgently in my head. Knowing that someone without strong abilities like mine would have trouble picking up what I was sending, I began to alternate repeating where we were with sending a mental image of where we were.

"Concrete bunker," Cash finally repeated and tears filled my eyes.

"He heard me. Oh my God, he heard me," I said, grabbing Trace's arms and shaking him in excitement.

"Yes!" Trace said, shooting his arm in the air.

"That doesn't solve the problem of Larry, Moe, and Curly on the patio though," I said. "Or how we are going to get out of this bunker."

"Do you think the breaking spell will work on the lock?"

Well, shoot.

I swear, give a girl all the tools and she's still bound to mess a few things up, am-I-right?

"Well, I suppose we can try," I said with a sniff, knowing my face was probably bright red.

"Can you tell how close Cash is?" Trace asked, having forgone calling him "that guy" for the moment.

I closed my eyes and reached out again.

"Thea, we are close to the island. Just out of view behind the point and hoping to stay off the radar. If you can make any sort of distraction, now's the time."

"He wants a distraction."

"Well, let's give him one."

"On it," I said, focusing my eyes on the door.

Undo this bond
  At once set us free
  As we must respond
  For our light is in need
  As I will, so mote it be.

The click of the lock falling from the door had to be one of the best sounds that I've ever heard in my life.

"Ready to run for it?" Trace asked, pulling me to a standing position.

"Let me take my flip-flops off," I said, sliding out of my sandals, and running my hands down my body to tuck my tank in. As my hand slid over my shorts, I remembered the pouch that Miss Elva had given me.

Just a tip here, I'm probably not the best person to get stuck in a crisis with.

Pulling the pouch out, I cupped it in my palm, praying that Miss Elva had meant what she had said about providing protection for me. Because we were about to hightail it across an open beach with three armed men trying to stop us.

"Clear?" I asked as Trace peeked out of the crack in the door.

"As much as I can see."

"Do it," I whispered and bit down hard on my lower lip when Trace whipped the door open. For a moment, I was blinded by the sudden wash of light as we had been sitting in the dark for so long, and I stumbled as we leapt from the bunker.

"To the dock," Trace shouted, and I squinted, my eyes adjusting to the light and seeing the most glorious sight I could have asked for.

A luxury speedboat, Cash at the helm and Beau with a machine gun at the front, was cruising up to dock.

Don't get me started on Beau holding a machine gun. I'm not sure which was scarier, him at the helm in his perfectly coordinated outfit or the three men who tore over the sand dune to block our path.

"Thea!" Trace shouted, just as Dupree raised his gun at my face.

"No!" I screeched and threw Miss Elva's pouch at their feet.

There was silence as the three men stopped for a second and stared at the pouch in confusion.

Ka-boom!

A scream tore from my throat as I raced past an explosion of smoke and noxious fumes that had me coughing into my hand, my eyes watering from the putrid smell. Refusing to look back, I ran side by side with Trace to the end of the dock where Cash held the boat to the dock with one hand.

"Jump!" Beau screamed and we both did, slipping and sliding our way across a cushy bench before we tumbled onto the floor.

"Hold on!' Cash shouted as he floored it, sending Trace and me rolling across the floor of the boat, staring up in awe as Beau fired off rounds at the beach. He looked magnificent and I swear if I'd had my phone on me, I'd have taken his picture.

I held my breath as the boat rocketed away from the shore, tears streaming down my face. Moments later, Cash cut the engine to slow us down a bit.

And I was promptly plucked from the floor and pulled into a bear hug by Cash. Shocked, I held on, my body trembling, and I pressed my cheek against his arm and looked back at where the island was fading in the distance. I could see the three men racing to their boat.

"They're coming after us," I said, straightening.

"No worries," Cash said, turning me so I could look out of the other side of the boat.

And there stood Chief Thomas at the helm of his Coast Guard boat, with at least ten police and FBI boats behind.

"I knew I liked him," I said, smiling and waving at Chief Thomas.

"Mmhm, so do I," Beau said, smiling cheekily at Chief Thomas in his uniform.

"I would suggest putting that illegal semi-automatic weapon down," Cash said gently and Beau jumped.

"Whoopsie," he said on a laugh, gently lowering the

gun to the bench and waving again. I saw Chief Thomas shake his head, but they had bigger fish to fry right now.

"This is the police!" a man shouted from the bullhorn and I saw the men on the beach scramble away from their boat and flee up to the house.

"There's seven people in there," I told Cash.

Nodding, he picked up his walkie-talkie and I saw Chief Thomas do the same on his end.

"Should we stay and help or something?" I asked and Cash looked down at me and laughed.

"I think we've all done enough. Cocktails on your porch in twenty minutes."

The man had read my mind.

Chapter Thirty-Two

BACK AT THE DOCKS, we stopped by where my bike was locked.

"I need to get my bike."

Cash looked at me like I had a screw loose, which, in all fairness, I probably do.

"We can throw it in my trunk," he said, stopping to look at me.

"No, I'd like to ride home."

"Yeah, 'cause the last time you rode away on your bike things went so well," Beau said, rolling his eyes.

"Hey, all the bad guys are back there on the island getting their asses handed to them," I said indignantly.

"Or so you think," Cash said.

"I just need to take care of something on the way home," I said.

"You've got twenty minutes or I'm coming after you," Cash warned, stopping to drop a kiss on my lips. I felt my cheeks heat and couldn't bring myself to look at Trace.

I waved to them as I swung onto my bike, feeling a little strange to be leaving the docks without my dive bag on my back, and pedaled my way down the street, pulling to the side halfway home and propping my bike against a front porch.

The light was low, the sun just setting, so it had been over twelve hours since I had last been here in the wee hours of the morning.

"Hmpf, looks like you did alright for yourself then," Miss Elva called from her porch and I shaded my eyes from the setting sun to look up at her.

"You should sell that little bag of tricks you got going on there," I said as I climbed the stairs to where she sat, rocking in her chair, no shotgun in sight.

"He, he, he," Miss Elva chortled, the mountain rumbling again as she laughed.

"Thank you," I said, bending down to wrap my arms around her, surprised to learn she smelled like cinnamon and vanilla. Pressing my lips to her cheek in a kiss, I squeezed one more time before letting her go.

"You're a good one, Miss Althea. I couldn't let you go without a few tricks up your sleeve."

"That was quite a trick," I agreed as I leaned back against the porch, crossing my arms as I studied her.

Miss Elva shrugged nonchalantly, but a pleased smile crossed her face.

"That had to have been the largest stink bomb I've ever seen," I said and the mountain rumbled again as Miss Elva slapped her knee and chuckled.

"So that's what it ended up being? You never do know," she said, wiping her eyes.

"You never know?" I squeaked, raising my eyebrows at her.

"I charmed it so it was what it needed to be," Miss Elva said.

"We needed a big distraction," I said and filled her in on the story. By the end of it, she was no longer laughing.

"Shoot, girl, I would have given you more pouches had I known you'd go and get into this much trouble."

"It all worked out. And I'm glad I can say that. I have to go now, we need to spring Luna," I said, never having thought that I would have to utter those words in my life.

"You give that girl a hug from me. Tell her to come see me. There's some things we can work on together," she said as I descended the wooden porch steps.

"Will do. If I could cook, you'd be getting a homemade apple pie. I like you too much to poison you though," I called, smiling as her chuckle followed me down the road.

It's good to have friends in all the right places.

Chapter Thirty-Three

HANK'S EARS POKED over the windowsill when I pulled up to my house. A happier sight I have never seen, I thought as I locked my bike to the porch and pushed the door open.

"Hey, buddy," I said, dropping to my knees and wrapping my arms around him as he licked my face in joy.

"Hey buddy yourself."

"Luna!" I shouted, springing up to rush across the room to where Luna stood by the breakfast counter. Launching myself at her, I wrapped my arms around her shoulders, never wanting to let go.

We squeezed each other, not saying anything, just letting the goodness flow before we pulled apart, both wiping happy tears.

"When I said find the killer, you didn't have to go and be all dramatic about it," she said, poking me in the shoulder.

"You know me – total drama queen," I said.

"Ladies? We stopped and got a gallon of my specialty

margarita mix and the ice is melting," Beau called from the patio.

Walking onto the patio, it felt like my heart was going to burst with happiness. Until I saw Trace. Holding ice to the bruise on his face, he sat across from Cash, looking everywhere but at him.

Looks like I had a few more loose ends to tie up, I thought. I wondered how this would all play out.

"Drink for you, my dear," Beau said, handing me a margarita on the rocks with a perfectly salted rim. I plopped onto the couch next to Cash, too tired to care if Trace took it the wrong way, and took a long slug of my drink.

"Still the best," I said, holding my drink up to Beau.

"Cheers," we all said, clinking our glasses.

"Okay, I have to know. How did you know where we were?" I asked, turning to Cash.

"Why don't you start at the beginning?" Beau interrupted, stopping Cash from answering my question.

"Well, I guess that starts with Trace," I said, gesturing to where he sat. "I got to the boat and Luca had already knocked him out."

"Luca," Beau said sadly, shaking his head.

"I know. It's awful," I said, turning to Luna. "By the way, you were right. Even though Theodore is a pompous twit, he just really loves his wife." I filled her in on the incident at the store, causing both Trace and Cash to shake their heads at me.

"What else happened?" Beau said quickly, moving past Theodore threatening me in the shop.

"Well, I can't say much," Trace said, detailing how he had climbed onto the boat with his hands full of gear and then it had been lights out until he woke up to see me sitting across from him on the floor of the boat. "I didn't even know it was Luca until I finally came to on the floor of the boat."

"And I saw your hand sticking out from the bench so I just rushed onto the boat without looking," I said, shrugging as Beau shook his head at me. "What? I don't always think straight."

"No kidding," Luna said.

"Hey!"

"So why did Luca do this?" Luna asked and I realized that I was the only one who knew Luca's story.

"Greed," I said sadly, taking another sip of my drink as I filled everyone in on the neat little drug operation they planned to run through his deli.

"I suppose that means the space is open for your restaurant," Cash mused, smiling at Beau.

"Oh yeah!" Beau sprang up and did a wiggle dance and then sat down, putting his serious face on. "I mean, how awful."

"Right," I said, laughing at Beau as he tried to look sad about the day's events.

"Back to my original question – how did you know where we were?"

A look of guilt crossed Cash's face and I raised an eyebrow at him.

"Um, hello?"

"I downloaded a location app onto your phone the other day. As long as it was on, I'd be able to find you."

"I like you," Beau said and I whipped my head around to glare at him.

"That's an invasion of my privacy."

"One that saved your butt. And I got to play with a big gun," Beau said gleefully, turning to Luna to tell her about his gun.

I sighed, rolling my eyes, and turned back to Cash.

"I'm not really okay with you doing that. But now I kind of have to be since you saved our lives."

"Well, you saved us, too." Trace spoke up and I turned to him, not sure what we could say in front of Cash.

Then again, who was I to hide anything? If the man wanted to date me, well, he'd better get real comfortable with the real me.

"The breaking spell worked," I said, turning to Luna, and she beamed at me.

"I knew it would. Thank God you listened to me for once and learned it."

Cash cleared his throat. "Breaking spell?"

"Luna's a white witch. We do spells sometimes," I said simply, watching his face for any reactions.

"Spells."

"Yes. In fact, she taught me a breaking spell that allowed me to not only break through our wrist zip-ties, but the door as well," I said cheerfully, leaning over to clink my glass against hers again.

"The door, too? Hmm, you may have more power than you realize, girl," Luna said thoughtfully.

"I do?" I said, tilting my head at her, having never considered that I might carry a little magic with me as well.

"You may. You've already got some considerable skills in other realms, so it wouldn't surprise me if you have a touch of magic too," she mused, pursing her lips as she thought about it.

"Magic," Cash repeated.

"Yup, magic. How cool is that?" I asked, daring him to say something negative.

"Somehow, this does not surprise me," he said on a sigh and then clinked his glass against mine, causing me to beam at him.

"Told you I liked him," Beau said.

"That guy," Trace muttered into his drink.

"That may explain that little explosion on the beach then." Cash frowned, leaning back to cross his arms across his broad chest. I couldn't help but drink in the view of his muscular arms as I looked at him.

"Yeah, what the heck was that?" Trace said, leaning forward to look at me.

"Miss Elva gave me a protection pouch. She told me to use it when I needed it," I said.

"You didn't think to use it earlier?" Trace said in disgust.

"It may have slipped my mind," I said, my nose in the air.

"Was it a bomb?" Beau asked.

"It, well, it turned out to be a really big stink bomb," I admitted and Luna snorted into her drink.

"I love that woman," she said as the others began to laugh.

"She wants to meet with you, by the way."

"I'll go to her this week."

"Hey! How did you get out of jail?"

"Ah, well, it seems the FBI got an anonymous tip with some email messages that were hacked from Dupree's account." Luna turned to raise her eyebrow at Cash who held up his hands in protest.

"I hope you aren't insinuating that I would hack into an officer of the law's account?" Cash asked.

"Not me," Beau said.

"Of course not," I said, fighting to keep a smile off my face.

Epilogue

AN HOUR LATER, Cash's phone beeped with an incoming message.

"They got them. All of them. They want me to come in to answer some questions now, and they'll need you guys at the station first thing tomorrow," Cash said, nodding his head toward Trace and me.

"Yay!" I shouted, deliriously happy that it had all worked out.

Beau looked around at all of us and then stood.

"Come on, Trace, Luna, I'll drop you two off on the way to the restaurant. I have some serious catching up to do," he said, standing and stretching. Bending over, he dropped a kiss on my cheek.

"Wait here," I said to Cash and followed them to my front door, stepping onto the porch and closing the door behind me.

"I'll go to the store tomorrow while you go to the station," Luna said, giving me another quick squeeze before following Beau to his car.

Trace turned to look at me and I smiled at him, reaching up to run my hand lightly over the bruise on his face.

"I'm sorry you got hurt," I said softly, bringing my hand down to my side.

"Not your fault," Trace said and then paused. His eyes met mine and my heart clenched a bit in my chest.

"That guy?" he said, gesturing with his thumb towards where Cash sat inside.

"Yes?"

"He's alright," he said.

"Oh, Trace," I said, incredibly sad but not knowing why.

"Hey, it's okay. We're friends first. Friends always. Tell him to stay on his toes though. Because I'll steal you in a heartbeat," Trace said softly, bending over to brush his lips softly over mine.

"Thanks, Trace," I whispered, clenching my lips together as he walked down the porch steps and hopped into the back seat of Beau's car. A cheerful honk from them propelled me back inside.

Suddenly nervous, I walked slowly back to where Cash stood by the counter. He'd cleaned up outside and was currently rinsing the glasses in the sink.

You had to love a guy who did the dishes, I thought, then mentally slapped myself for saying the word love. There was no love. Not yet at, least. As I eyed him up while he smiled at me over the sink, I realized that for once, though, there was a strong potential.

"All good?" he asked.

"Oh yeah, so good," I said, leaning on the counter next to him.

"Listen," Cash said as he wiped his hands on a towel and turned to stand in front of me, his arms caging me at the counter.

"Yes?" I asked, tilting my face up to him in a smile. Lord, was this man devastating.

"I have to go back to Miami tomorrow. One of my clubs has had a series of break-ins. I'll be back soon. And when I do, I'm coming for you, Althea Rose."

"I'll take your word for it," I said, my voice full of challenge, leaning in as he slid his lips over mine, heating me with just his touch.

Oh yeah. I was doomed.

Afterword

Thank you for taking a chance on my books; it means the world to me.

I hope my books add a little magick into your life. If you have a moment to add some to my day, you can help by telling your friends and leaving a review. Word-of-mouth is the most powerful way to share my stories. Thank you.

Unsurprisingly, I spend a lot of time underwater because I moved to the Caribbean to do just that. I have a very deep love for scuba-diving, and when I'm not writing I like to disappear into the ocean to take joy in the beauty that can be found there. I'm passionate about the conservation of coral reefs, and I love sharing this passion with my readers – both through my books and my scuba-diving photos that I share. I think a part of me has always dreamed of being a mermaid, as being underwater is a soothing and meditative experience for me. I hope my love for the ocean, my belief in the mystical, and my hope that fairy tales really can come true rings through for you in my books. Thanks for taking a peek into my world with me.

If you enjoy looking at scuba-diving photos, island pictures, puppy photos, and the occasional pictures of a hot Scotsman – be sure to sign up for my newsletter at www.-triciaomalley.com

Available as an e-book, paperback or audiobook!

The following is an excerpt from
Tequila For Two
Book 2 in the Althea Rose Mystery Series

Chapter One

"WHAT'S UP WITH THAT?" I asked, straining my eyes at the line of people approaching our shop.

"Pagan festival this weekend." Luna shrugged her delicate shoulders, tucking a strand of her wispy blonde hair behind her ear. Clad in a white linen dress and with the highest cheekbones I had ever seen, Luna was all elegance and grace. If I were casting for a white witch in a play, she would fit the part perfectly.

In more ways than looks.

Me, on the other hand? Well, I'm more curvy than Luna with the grace of an elephant, I suppose. This past month I'd darkened the hot pink streaks in my curls to more of a deep lavender color, and white clothes and I do not mix – mainly because I don't corner well and have a habit of spilling things on myself.

"Friends of yours?" I asked, knowing that as a white witch – yes, a real one – Luna had some roots in Paganism.

"Not that I'm aware of," Luna hummed, raising a delicate eyebrow.

"How did we not know there was a Pagan festival this weekend?"

Luna shrugged. "It was in the weekly paper."

"You know I've sworn off the paper after Craig wrote up that article about you," I said. A month ago Luna had been falsely accused of murder, and even though we'd threatened the local reporter with some pretty inventive curses, he'd still written a fairly accusatory article about Luna. A small retraction printed in the paper after Luna was cleared of all charges had done little to change my opinion of him.

"We still need to think up a curse for him," Luna reminded me.

"I've got Miss Elva on it," I said, referring to our resident voodoo priestess. I trusted her implicitly to find the best revenge for this particular situation.

"That should do it," Luna agreed, pasting a smile on her face, as the line of people grew closer to our shop.

My name's Althea Rose and I, together with Luna, run the Luna Rose Potions & Tarot Shop.

She's the witch; I'm the psychic.

I can't help it – being a psychic runs in the blood. My mother is far more prolific than I, flitting from country to country to cater to the famous people she deems worthy of her readings. Oh, she's a diva, that's for sure. Most people would probably say I have a fair share of her attitude, but I like to think that I take after my easygoing musician father, who has happily followed my mother on her travels.

Luna snorted. "Easygoing, my ass," she murmured, her polite smile never faltering.

"Stop reading my mind," I grumbled, moving from the

white-and-gold upscale beach-cottage elegance of her side of the shop to the velvety purple den of iniquity on my side.

Okay, so maybe "den of iniquity" is taking it a little far. But my tarot card shop was exactly what you would presume one to be – there was even a leopard-print chair tucked away in a corner.

And a skeleton wearing a Ramones shirt was sitting on it.

Pulling out my phone, I reluctantly googled the local paper to find out more about this Pagan festival. Tequila Key wasn't exactly known to be a hot spot for festivals. Or for anything, for that matter.

We are a sleepy little Key, just a speed bump for tourists on their way to Key West. Most people simply pulled to the side of the road to snap a picture by the "Tequila Makes it Better" sign that some genius had erected by the marker off the highway before continuing on down to a livelier Key. Any sort of festival was bound to be the talk of the town.

"The New Crusaders, a revolutionized order of the Pagan druids," I read out loud, raising an eyebrow at my screen. "Sounds like radicals."

"Some may call us that," said a voice to my left, and I jumped. I hadn't realized that someone had slipped past my privacy screen to wait politely at the entrance to my shop.

At least six feet tall and rail thin, a man who reminded me of Gandalf stood at my door. His hair and beard flowed in long gray waves over his forest green ritual cloak, and his feet were encased in butter-smooth leather boots.

That explained why I hadn't heard his entrance.

"Hello," I said, unaccountably wary.

"Hello. I wanted to see if I could arrange readings for some of my group this weekend."

"I'd have to check my schedule," I said, pointedly not reaching for my schedule. Something about this man's vibe was making me reluctant to help him.

"I'll wait," he said with a smile.

"What's your name?"

"I am Horace, the founding member, and the organizer of this weekend's festival," Horace said.

"And what is this festival for, exactly?"

"Why, to celebrate the earth, the sky, the ocean...all the natural beauty of this place. And this weekend is the full moon which also coincides with the equinox. We'll be celebrating the Mabon festival, to prepare us for the darker time of the year," Horace said, sweeping his hand around in a grand gesture.

I swear his eyes seemed to light up when he talked about the "darker time of the year." And what was he doing wearing a ritual cloak outside of an actual ritual? Even I knew that's frowned upon.

"In Tequila Key? Granted, we've got a stunning coastline, but we are a fairly cluttered little town, if you hadn't noticed."

"You've some lovely natural spaces outside of town for us to set up in. There's a private campground that we've rented out. You're welcome to come. In fact, I insist," Horace said gravely.

"I'll get back to you on that one, Horace. I'm sorry, but I have a telephone appointment at eleven. I'll be sure to let you know about my availability this weekend. Cheers," I said, smiling brightly and reached for my phone.

Horace held my gaze for a moment, his eyes so light a grey that they were almost white, before nodding once and padding silently from my room in his leather booties.

And leaving me with an unsettled feeling as I picked up my phone to call my client.

Available from Amazon

The Althea Rose Series

ALSO BY TRICIA O'MALLEY

One Tequila

Tequila for Two

Tequila Will Kill Ya (Novella)

Three Tequilas

Tequila Shots & Valentine Knots (Novella)

Tequila Four

A Fifth of Tequila

A Sixer of Tequila

Seven Deadly Tequilas

Eight Ways to Tequila

Available in audio, e-book & paperback!

Available from Amazon

"Not my usual genre but couldn't resist the Florida Keys setting. I was hooked from the first page. A fun read with just the right amount of crazy! Will definitely follow this series."- Amazon Review

Ms. Bitch

FINDING HAPPINESS IS THE BEST REVENGE

You'll laugh, you'll cry, and you'll cheer for Tess on her way to living her best life. Grab this summer's hottest beach read – it pairs well with a margarita and flip-flops!

Read Today

"Ms. Bitch is sunshine in a book! An uplifting story of fighting your way through heartbreak and making your own version of happily-ever-after."

~Ann Charles, USA Today Bestselling Author of the Deadwood Mystery Series

"Authentic and relatable, Ms. Bitch packs an emotional punch. By the end, I was crying happy tears and ready to pack my bags in search of my best life."
-Annabel Chase, author of the Starry Hollow Witches series

"I don't know where to start listing all the reasons why you should read this book. It's empowering. It's fierce. It's about loving yourself enough to build the life you want. It was honest, and raw, and real and I just...loved it so much!"
— Sara Wylde, author of Fat

One Way Ticket

A PERFECT ROMANTIC BEACH READ

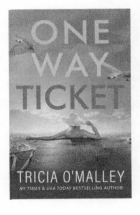

Tricia's latest romance is a funny and heart-pounding story where booking a one-way ticket to paradise means starting over, letting go, and taking a chance on love.

Read Today

The Isle of Destiny Series

ALSO BY TRICIA O'MALLEY

Stone Song

Sword Song

Spear Song

Sphere Song

Available in audio, e-book & paperback!

Available from Amazon

"Love this series. I will read this multiple times. Keeps you on the edge of your seat. It has action, excitement and romance all in one series."- Amazon Review

The Siren Island Series

ALSO BY TRICIA O'MALLEY

Good Girl

Up to No Good

A Good Chance

Good Moon Rising

Too Good To Be True

A Good Soul

Available in audio, e-book & paperback!

Available from Amazon

"Love her books and was excited for a totally new and different
one! Once again, she did NOT disappoint! Magical in multiple
ways and on multiple levels. Her writing style, while similar to
that of Nora Roberts, kicks it up a notch!! I want to visit that
island, stay in the B&B and meet the gals who run it! The
characters are THAT real!!!" - Amazon Review

Contact Me

Love books? What about fun giveaways? Nope? Okay, can I entice you with underwater photos and cute dogs? Let's stay friends, receive my emails by signing up at my website

www.triciaomalley.com

As always, you can reach me at
info@triciaomalley.com

Or find me on Facebook and Instagram.
@triciaomalleyauthor

Author's Acknowledgement

First, and foremost, I'd like to thank my family and friends for their constant support, advice, and ideas. You've all proven to make a difference on my path. And, to my beta readers, I love you for all of your support and fascinating feedback!

And last, but never least, my two constant companions as I struggle through words on my computer each day - Briggs and Blue.

Made in the USA
Coppell, TX
31 March 2025

47725664R00152